Acclaim for Arthur Bradford and

Dogwalker

"It's nice, for a change, to see violence disarmed, pain anesthetized, and the alien rendered cuddly."
—*Los Angeles Times*

"Arthur Bradford's stories are quite simply the mutt's nuts: One of the funniest, smartest, tallest writers at work in America today."
—Zadie Smith

"Bradford's fiction envisions a world where anything can happen or can have happened. . . . He's careful not to make it explicit, but the subtext of *Dogwalker* is tender to the point of sentimentality." —*The Village Voice*

"Anyone who's ever wondered at the weirdness of the world will be grateful for these offerings."
—*Entertainment Weekly*

"Bradford never fails to surprise, and even to shock." —*The Washington Post Book World*

ARTHUR BRADFORD

Dogwalker

Arthur Bradford's fiction has appeared in *McSweeney's*, *Esquire*, and *The O. Henry Awards*. He is also the creator and director of *How's Your News?*, a traveling news show produced by the denizens of Camp Jabberwocky, the oldest camp for adults with disabilities in the country.

Every thought you have creates its own reality . . .
—*Richard Linklater,* Slacker

Dogwalker

Stories by

ARTHUR BRADFORD

Vintage Contemporaries
Vintage Books
A Division of Random House, Inc.
New York

To my mother, father, and my twin sister, Laura

FIRST VINTAGE CONTEMPORARIES EDITION, AUGUST 2002

Copyright © 2001, 2002 by Arthur Bradford

Some of the stories in this collection were originally published in different form in *Bomb, Epoch, Esquire, Index, McSweeney's,* and *Speak.*

Vintage is a registered trademark and Vintage Contemporaries and colophon are trademarks of Random House, Inc.

The Library of Congress has cataloged the Knopf edition as follows:
Dogwalker : stories / by Arthur Bradford. — 1st ed.
p.   cm.
Contents: Catface — Mollusks — The Texas School for the Blind — South for the winter — Mattress — The house of Alan Matthews — Six dog Christmas — Bill McQuill — Little Rodney — Chainsaw apple — Dogs — Roslyn's dog.
ISBN 0-375-41232-8 — ISBN 0-375-72669-1 (pbk.)
1. Eccentrics and eccentricities—Fiction.
2. Humorous stories, American. I. Title.
PS3602.R34 D64 2001
813'.6—dc21   2001029769

Vintage ISBN: 0-375-72669-1

Drawings by Katherine Bradford

www.vintagebooks.com

Printed in the United States of America
10   9   8   7   6   5   4   3   2   1

Contents

Acknowledgments

Thank you (in no particular order): Matthew Baxter, Maggie Vining, Dave Eggers, John Hodgman, Kassie Evashevski, Jordan Pavlin, Adrienne Miller and David Granger at *Esquire*, John L'Heureux, Michael Koch at *Epoch*, Denis Johnson, The Texas Center for Writers, Lars Eighner, Chad Urmston, Kerry Glamsch, Larry Dark, Zadie Smith, Oscar Van Gelderen, Carol Noyes, Susan Bradford, Anita Houston, Timothy McSweeney and friends, Creston Lea, Agnes Krup, the How's Your News Crew, Camp Jabberwocky, and a shout out to my little sister Emily.

And very grateful acknowledgment to the James Michener and Wallace Stegner Fellowship programs.

Dogwalker

Catface

The disability payments were being cut down since, according to their doctor, I was getting better. I had been without work for months and needed money so I decided to share my place and split the cost. My place was small. They called it a "studio apartment," which meant it had only one room. The kitchen was set off in the corner and my little bed sat over against the opposite wall. It was a cozy arrangement.

My first roommate was a guy named Thurber. He breathed very heavily through his nose and when he spoke the words came out in high-pitched squeaks. Thurber moved quickly with jerks and twists like spasms and for a while I thought he was diseased. He had dark circles under his eyes. Before he moved in I had placed two small green plants on the windowsill but once Thurber saw those he pitched them out the window. "Damn plants!" he yelled after them. Later on I brought in a larger banana plant and he screamed at me, "Get that fucking plant out of here!"

Thurber had answered my ad for roommate-wanted by showing up at my door with his bags. I am a somewhat meek person and I let him stay even though I was suspicious of his shifty appearance. Thurber said he was a good cook and would prepare fine meals for me. I said, great, I like good food as much as the next guy. As it turned out Thurber hardly ever cooked and when he did he made a chaotic mess which sat there for days until I cleaned it up myself. Thurber's taste in food was always too hot for my palate and his dishes usually looked nothing like whatever he said they were supposed to be. "This is Lemon Chicken," he once said. But the food in question looked more like baked beans, or maybe some kind of Sloppy Joe.

Thurber snored loudly, too, and this was finally why he had to leave. "Thurber," I said, "you snore like a pig and I can't sleep. Perhaps you should find somewhere else to go."

"I don't snore," replied Thurber, but he left the next afternoon. As he packed up his stuff he casually slipped several pieces of my clothing into his bag. He also took a brand-new toothbrush of mine and a large lamp. I was standing right there watching him.

My next roommate was a woman named Cynthia who claimed to have some children whom she kept at her sister's house. I never saw them. Cynthia read three or four magazines a day and it wasn't until a few weeks of living with her that I learned about her hooking business. When I was gone she would take men into our place and give them head for ten to twenty dollars apiece. According to her she never had real sex with them and I'm inclined to believe this because I have been in whore-houses before and they have a certain electricity to them. It's in the air. I never felt this electric feeling when I walked into my home. A man who lived next door told me about all the male visitors and so that night I said to Cynthia, "What's going on here?"

She said, "Oh, I just give them blow jobs for money."

After Cynthia, Clyde moved in and he stayed for only three days. He had a large duffel bag full of clothes but he never changed outfits once since I knew him. He liked his blue jeans and T-shirt, I guess. Two guys with tooth-picks in their mouths showed up on Clyde's third day and they stood in the doorway staring at Clyde for quite some time before one said, "Let's go, Clyde."

Jimmy moved in next and he was a real card. He told jokes to me all the time and some of them were very funny. I remember one in particular about a rabbit working in a gas station which had me laughing off and on for hours.

"You should be a comedian Jimmy," I once said.

"That's what they all say," he said.

As far as I could tell, Jimmy helped out a man who took bets on college sporting events. I'm not nosy and I don't pry into the lives of other people. Jimmy had simply told me that he was "in sports management."

I appreciated Jimmy's sense of humor a lot and then one day Jimmy did something which made me appreciate him even more. He brought in a small orange tent and set it up right inside the apartment. He put his blankets and pillow in there and said, "See, this way I have my own room."

Jimmy and his tent had been in the apartment for nearly two months when we heard a loud knock on the door.

"It's me, Thurber," said the voice behind the door. It was high-pitched, whining even.

"Come on in, Thurber," I said, but I did not get up to open the door for him.

Thurber rattled the handle a little bit and then whacked the door with his hand. It was locked. I still didn't get up and so after a while he went away.

Jimmy said, "I know some friends who could kick that guy's ass."

"That would be nice," I said.

———

A few days later Thurber came into our apartment. He let himself in with a set of keys he had kept from before. His lip was fat and purple and both his eyes were black.

"I need to wash up," he said.

Thurber limped over to the sink and splashed water all over the place. "A group of men kicked my ass for no reason," he said.

"If you had keys," I said, "why didn't you let yourself in earlier?"

"I never even met those fuckers before in my life." Thurber was covered in water, pink from his own blood. He looked terrible. His hair was greasy and his clothing was matted with dirt.

"You look terrible," I said.

Thurber spied a group of potted plants by the window and lunged at them. His skinny arm knocked them over and the dirt spilled onto the carpet.

"Why is there a tent in here?" he asked me.

Jimmy answered him from inside. "It's my tent, asshole," he said.

Thurber looked down at the tent which had just spoken to him.

"You're kidding me," he said.

"No, I'm not," said Jimmy's voice. "And those were my friends who kicked your ass. I asked them to do it."

Thurber was amazed. He stumbled around and stuttered a bit and then walked out the door. He left drops of water all over the place and a putrid smell which lingered in the air for a while. The plants lay overturned on the carpet.

"Keep me posted on any developments with this Thurber fruitcake," said Jimmy one day as he packed his bag.

"I'm going away for a while so I won't be around," he said.

"Okay, fine," I said, and then that day I found myself a pet dog. I didn't know how long Jimmy would be away and so I wanted some company. I have always wanted a dog.

The dog I found had only three legs. He was missing a front one so he hopped forward on one paw. Like most three-legged dogs this dog managed quite well for himself and I didn't feel sorry for him at all. While Jimmy was gone the dog and I went out for frequent walks and once I got a citation for not having a leash on my pet.

"I'm really sorry about this officer," I said. "It will never happen again." And I meant that. I want no trouble with the law. I used a piece of rope instead of a leash though.

Once when the dog and I returned from a walk we found Thurber sitting inside the apartment with a man we all knew as "Catface." Catface was a guy who had some sort of medical problem which made his face very shiny and flat. His eyes were only little slits. His nose was small and flattened and his ears were tiny and crumpled up. I had once thought that Catface was the victim of a bad accident with fire but then someone told me that this was not the case. He was born like that.

"Hello, Thurber," I said, "Hello, Catface." We all called him Catface. There was no hiding it.

Thurber, I noticed, had been eating my food. It was in a bowl next to where he sat. The funny thing about it was he had chosen some food I had intended to feed to the dog.

"You've eaten the dog's food," I said.

Thurber said, "Your dog only has three legs."

"I know that," I said.

"Where's the guy who lives in the tent?" asked Thurber.

I hadn't noticed this before but now I saw that stupid Thurber had dismantled Jimmy's tent and scattered it all over the floor.

"Oh, you shouldn't have done that," I said. I looked at Catface to see if he too had been part of the destruction.

"If he had been inside that thing he would have been in a lot of trouble," said Thurber. "Catface would have tore him apart."

Catface nodded in agreement.

"Listen," I said, "I wish you two hadn't come in here and messed up Jimmy's stuff. Now we have to clean it up before he gets back."

"Where is he?" asked Thurber.

"I don't know," I answered.

Thurber and Catface decided to leave. On the way out Catface patted my dog.

"How are you, Catface?" I asked. I hadn't seen him in a while. In fact, I had never spoken to him before, but I think he knew who I was.

"I'm doing okay," said Catface.

When Jimmy returned a few days later he didn't notice what Thurber and Catface had done because I had cleaned up the mess. He laid his stuff down on a chair and said to me, "I'd like you to meet my friend Robyn."

In walked this woman with straight red hair and a large ring through the tip of her nose.

"That's a nice ring," I said.

Robyn said, "Thank you."

I introduced Jimmy and Robyn to the dog and Jimmy told a joke about a three-legged dog who ran a Laundromat. After he was done and we all chuckled Jimmy said, "Robyn and I are going to step out for a while."

They didn't get back until it was almost morning and the dog barked loudly when they walked in. Robyn made a hissing sound through her teeth which shut him up right away.

It wasn't until late in the afternoon that Jimmy and

Robyn crawled out of the tent. Robyn was completely naked and I saw that she had several tattoos, including one of a wicked snake which coiled up her thigh. Again the dog barked at them and again Robyn hissed. I found my piece of rope and took the dog for a walk so as to give Jimmy and Robyn some time to themselves.

We wandered around for hours and didn't get back until after dark. Inside the apartment I discovered that Robyn and Jimmy had lit about a hundred candles. The candles were melting and wax was dripping everywhere. I could feel the heat.

"This is something else," I said.

Jimmy and Robyn were sitting on my bed. "I heard about what that fuckface Thurber did to my tent," said Jimmy.

"I haven't seen him since that," I said.

"Robyn has placed a hex on him," said Jimmy. "His life will never be the same."

I was not let in on the specifics of Robyn's hex. I knew only that it involved many candles and would eventually make Thurber very miserable.

"Is it working?" I asked Robyn after a few days had passed.

"Oh, yes," she said, and then she muttered something about how "all sheep do cometh yonder."

"Do you worship Satan?" I asked her.

"No, I do not," she said.

Jimmy and Robyn decided to go out one afternoon and I was instructed to keep the candles burning. They had been gone only about ten minutes when Thurber burst in. He looked worse than I had ever seen him. He was sweaty and his teeth were black.

"And what is going on here?" he yelled.

"Hello, Thurber," I said.

"What is this voodoo bullshit? Huh?"

"Jimmy's friend Robyn is interested in this," I said. The dog growled at Thurber. I had never seen someone so close to death. Thurber's skin was a pale green. He had lost weight and his ratty clothes were falling off of him.

Thurber began knocking the candles over with wild sweeps of his thin arms. I was worried he would start a fire. He soon became winded though and had to stop.

"Jimmy will be upset about this," I said.

Thurber coughed and collapsed onto the floor. I went over to his smelly body and saw that he was still breathing. I dragged him out the door, down the stairs, and onto the street where I left him lying.

At some point Thurber must have gotten up and left because Jimmy and Robyn did not see him on their way in. They did however see the waxy mess he had left behind when he knocked over the candles. Robyn exclaimed, "He hath come."

———

That night Robyn spent several hours smearing paint and makeup all over Jimmy's body. When she was done Jimmy looked like an animal of the jungle.

"Go forth," she said to Jimmy. "Seek ye the lamb."

Jimmy walked out the door naked, covered in the paint of many colors.

"What is a person going to think when they see that?" I asked.

Robyn placed a finger over her lip and said, "Shhh . . ."

We waited up for Jimmy but dawn came and he did not return. Robyn let the candles die out.

"My work is done here," she said to me.

"Where is Jimmy?" I asked.

"He shall never return."

Robyn searched in her bag and produced a piece of fruit. It was dark, as if it had been ripe too long.

"Here," she said, holding the fruit out to me. "Eat of this and ye shall transcend."

It was a strange fruit, long and wrinkled. On its skin there were tiny hairs. I ate it and it tasted good.

I went walking with the dog in the early morning. The air was cold and I had to face away from the sun as it rose up. It was too bright. We limped along, me and the three-legged dog. I was feeling better. On the empty street I came across Catface. He too was wandering around.

"Hello Catface," I said.

"I understand you are looking for a roommate," said Catface.

"Yes I am," I said.

PART II
MUTANTS

I took my three-legged dog for a walk in the park today. He is a happy dog in spite of his lack of a front leg. He gets along just fine. When we go out, someone usually comes up to me and wants to know how it happened. I don't know the real answer but often I come up with some good tales about how a bear nipped it off in the woods or how when he was a puppy he got too close to a bandsaw. The truth is I got him this way. He was limping around outside my place and I took him in. I was lonely at the time (I still am) and I figured I needed a pet.

So today I was walking with him and this woman approached me with very wide eyes. She said, "Hey, you've got a dog with only three legs."

I said, "That's right."

The woman kept looking at me from different angles, like she wasn't sure if I was really there, as if maybe

I was a mirage or an illusion. She said, "I too have a dog."

"With three legs?" I inquired.

"No," she said, "she's got all four."

Just then a chubby little hound waddled up to us with her tail wagging and her tongue hanging out. "This is Esmerelda," said the woman.

"Nice name," I said.

We watched together as Esmerelda and my three-legged dog frolicked about on the grass. That Esmerelda sure was a flirt!

Then I turned to the lady and asked, "Is your dog fixed?" By that I meant had the dog been given an operation so that it could no longer reproduce.

The woman said, "Oh, no. Of course not. Do you believe in that?"

"Oh, I don't know," I said. I didn't know. Perhaps we should leave our dogs alone, let them breed as they please.

The dogs were getting along famously. They licked and bit and clawed and chomped at each other's faces.

"This is nice that they are playing," I said.

"Yes," said the woman. I then got a close look at her. I wouldn't mind being with her, I thought. She had a soft face with a kind of European look to it, possibly Polish. Her eyes were sad and she had brown curly hair. She was no looker, to be sure, but I would have all the same.

She then asked me, "Do you know a lot about dogs?"

"Well, I know a little bit," I said, "about as much as anyone else."

"Esmerelda has had some puppies," she said. "Would you like to see them?"

I said, "Yes, I would." Puppies!

The woman led me back to her small apartment. It looked out over an enormous parking lot. She said the lights from the lot shined in her windows at night so that the whole place sort of glowed.

"Must be hard to sleep," I ventured.

"Yes, it is," she said, after giving it some thought.

She took me to a little back room where the puppies were strewn about on the floor. It was dark in there because she had hung a bedsheet over the window. Esmerelda wandered in and lay down among the squirming mass. Tiny whimpers rose into the air, little sniffles and cries of recognition. My dog stood cautiously behind us in the doorway.

"How about turning on a light?" I said. I couldn't see the little critters. They only appeared to be lumps of fur.

Before she flicked on the light switch the woman said to me, "Now, I think there might be something wrong with them . . ."

What an understatement that was. The little pups were mutants! Deformed! They crawled about on mere nubs instead of legs. Several were missing limbs altogether. Three of them were attached at the sides—three-way Siamese twins.

I stood there dumbfounded. What a collection of misfits!

"These puppies are deformed," I finally said. One of them had no eyes. Where the sockets should have been there was just skin, flat and covered with fur. What strange creature had Esmerelda come across?

The woman looked at me, worried. "I know they are wrong," she said, "I know most puppies don't come out like that. I already knew that."

My dog began a low growl from behind us. "Grrrrrrr," he said. Esmerelda just lay among them, a proud mother.

"Well," I said, "I don't know what to tell you. I don't think some of them will survive." One forlorn pup had squirmed his way into a corner of the room. He was equipped with a set of four furry fins instead of legs. Flippers, maybe, like those of a sea tortoise.

The low *grrrrrrr* sound from behind us continued. I decided to step aside so that my dog could examine the mutants himself. He growled louder but ventured forth into the bodies all the same.

"Your dog," said the woman, "is abnormal also." She looked at me for some sort of confirmation, as if knowledge of this fact shared would ease her soul.

And I said, "Yes, this is true."

I reached out and took her hand, soft and clammy, into mine. She gripped me tight. My dog wandered among the whimpering pups, sniffing at them, on occasion giving one a gentle lick. I moved closer to the woman. I still didn't know her name. I put my arm around her and felt her bony shoulders. A nice warmth arose from them.

"Do you want to go into the other room?" I asked.

She nodded and we left the dogs to their sniffing and their strange little grunts and squeaks. We went into her bedroom and there I removed her clothing, half expecting to find some gross scar or hidden limb beneath it all. She was normal, though, with white skin and funny ribs which stuck out, making her look more slender than she really was. I sucked on her nipple and she let out a little moan, high-pitched, surprised, and excited.

PART III

CATFACE AND THE LITTLE DOGS

I had been living with Catface for a few weeks now. He kept strange hours, preferring to sleep during the day and leaving me alone at night. I'm not sure what he did with himself while he was away. He was employed part-time down at one of the warehouses, as a security guard, I believe. I had taken to visiting my woman friend Christine in the daytime, while he slept. Christine lived by herself with that room full of mutant puppies. Each morning I would make my way over there with my three-legged dog and we would tend to the little creatures. They needed constant care and supervision. Some of the more able pups had grown feisty and they were giving the others trouble, shutting them out from Esmerelda's milking breasts and nipping at their help-less nubs in a cruel mockery of puppy play. I suggested separating them but Christine would not have it. "They are a family," she said.

One day I returned to the apartment and Catface was singing in his sleep. It was a song about a cottontail rab-bit named Squeak. I had at first assumed that Catface was awake as he sung this tune but when I moved closer I saw that his little cat eyes were shut. He wore an imp-ish grin and his voice was pitched in a high falsetto, like a girl's. This is how the ditty went:

> "Oh, I am a cottontail rabbit named Squeak
> and I hop and play all day.
> Everywhere I go
> the kids are sure to follow
> because Squeak is here to stay!"

What a songbird that Catface was! I had never seen him so animated. He swung his round head from side to side in joyful exuberance as he chirped away. I took his singing as a sign that he had grown comfortable here and I was pleased about that.

When Catface woke up it was dark. He rubbed his little slits-for-eyes and gazed about the room.

"How's Squeak?" I asked him.

"What?" he said.

I began to sing his little song: *"Oh, I am a cottontail rabbit named Squeak and I hop and play all day . . ."*

Catface seemed confused. "What the hell is that?" he asked.

Was he really unaware of his own childish banter? Perhaps he was embarrassed. I decided to let it drop. I said, "Oh, it's nothing."

"Okay, fine," said Catface. He rose up from his bed, fully clothed, as was his habit. He did occasionally change his outfits but never before he went to sleep. He even kept his socks on. That night he was wearing what is known as "double denim"—blue jeans and a blue-jean shirt. He was a stylish person.

Catface stretched out his long arms and he said, "My family is coming to town."

"Oh, really?" I said. I didn't know Catface had any relatives at all, much less a whole family.

"They are coming through town on business," he said. "They'll be here for a few days."

"Excellent," I said. "Can I meet them?"

"Yes, you may," said Catface.

I wanted to ask him if they too possessed catfaces, but I felt it would be inappropriate. I would find out soon enough.

———

Esmerelda was growing weary of the constant nipping and tugging from her puppies. One day she got up and walked away from them, causing a great deal of commotion in the puppy room. They yipped and barked until we went in there ourselves with bottles of milk in hand. Christine had named the puppies after the Greek gods. I couldn't keep them all straight. There was Hermes with the furry flippers and there was Adonis with no eyes. There was Aphrodite with a cyclops eye and Athena with the nubs for legs. The three-way Siamese twins were simply called "The Weird Sisters" after the three witches in the play by Shakespeare called *MacBeth*.

The little mutants were growing larger and soon they would have to do without their mother's milk. "What plans do you have for these puppies?" I asked Christine.

She said, "I believe God has delivered them to me. I have accepted it as my mission to care for them all."

What a notion! This woman was going to live out her life with a dozen mutant dogs. I had, in more private moments, envisioned a happy future for Christine and myself. A small house in the country, perhaps, with that frisky Esmerelda and my three-legged dog, and maybe one or two of the mutants. But the whole lot of them? I began to question my fanciful dreams.

When I got home that day Catface was at it again with his singing. I said to myself, "I've got to get some proof of this." So I went down to my neighbor's place and borrowed his small tape recorder. I taped Catface singing, *"Oh, I am Squeak the cottontail. Won't you come and play with me?"* He sang it over and over.

That night, when Catface woke up, I said to him, "Boy, do I have something for you."

I played the tape for him and he said, "What the fuck is that?"

I said, "It's you singing."

"No, it's not," he said.

"Don't you remember this song?" I asked him. I turned up the volume on the tape player. It sounded ridiculous, like a psychotic young child.

Catface said, "Is this your idea of a joke?"

I gave up and turned off the tape player. "It's not a joke," I said. "It's you." I went downstairs to return the tape player to my neighbor, but I kept the tape for myself.

When I got back upstairs Christine and Esmerelda were in the apartment. Christine was sobbing and Catface had his hand on her shoulder in a comforting gesture. Christine looked up at me and she said, "The puppies are gone. Someone has taken them."

"That's awful," I said. "Why would someone do that?"

"I wish you had told me they were special puppies," said Catface. "I just wish I had known about that."

"I'm sorry," I said. "I thought I'd told you."

"Well, you didn't."

It occurred to me then that Catface and Christine had never met. I said, "Catface, this is Christine."

"I know that," said Catface.

Christine wiped her eyes with a hanky which Catface had given her. She said, "And you didn't tell me that Gerard had a catface."

I looked at Catface. "Your name is Gerard?" I asked.

"Yes, it is," he said.

We all sat down together and tried to think of what to do about the missing puppies. Catface and Christine seemed unusually comfortable with one another. At several points he boldly took her frail hands in his. I wondered if they were forming some kind of allegiance against me because I had not informed them of each other's mutation secrets.

We filed a police report and posted notices all over the neighborhood. They said, in big block letters, "WHO STOLE THE PUPPIES?" The intruder had left Christine's apartment a mess. He had rifled through everything, but the only objects he ended up stealing were the puppies, all twelve of them. I imagined this must have been quite a caper. Christine's clothes were scattered about everywhere and, in a particularly eerie touch, the houseplants had been uprooted and flung against the walls.

"Do you suppose Thurber is back in town?" I asked Catface.

"I think it is possible," he said.

That night Catface, Christine, and I took a bus out to the fairgrounds to see Catface's family. It turned out they were working for a traveling carnival. Catface said only that they "worked in the show," so I couldn't be sure what that meant. As we walked onto the fairgrounds Christine and Catface held hands and I tried to ignore that.

The carnival was lit up in a spectacular display of lighting technology. The rides soared toward the heavens glistening with robust colors and magical sounds. There were shouts and screams coming from all directions and the wind carried with it a distinct odor of sugar and flaming beef. I hadn't been to such an event since I was a small child and I must confess I was struck with awe.

Catface took it all in stride, however, and he led us calmly through the masses. He seemed suddenly at home in this land of glitz and grandeur. We walked by the Pickled Punk Show, a tent which claimed to have the bodies of freak babies preserved in jars. "There's no real flesh in there," said Catface. "It's just photographs. They outlawed the jars years ago."

Christine said, "I see."

For a dollar we could have entered a tent where a

man stuffed a python down his throat. There was a man who could hammer six-inch nails into the nostrils of his nose. There was a fire-eater and a sword-swallower and, of course, there was a fat lady. Catface led us past them all. "It's all real," he said.

We entered a small red tent pitched behind the hubbub and commotion. Catface went in first and he was greeted with cries of, "Gerard! Hooray, it's Gerard!" I followed Christine and watched as a whole family of them mobbed around my friend Catface. Yes, they had catfaces, too. There was the big papa, sitting in his chair, shiny flat face and all. There was the mama, plump as well, with her hair done up in a bun so that you could see her little crumpled ears. "How nice that they found each other," I thought. The kids, four of them, dashed about with enormous grins on their little catfaces. They leapt upon their big brother and showered him with love. "Gerard is here! Gerard is here!" they cried out. Of course they did not call him "Catface" as I had foolishly expected.

Catface introduced Christine and me to his jovial family and we all sat down for some tea. Mama Catface poured the potent brew and it tasted like nothing I had ever drunk before. "This is delicious," I said.

"Why, thank you," she said.

It turned out that Catface's family ran this show. Far from being freaks on display, as I had crassly hypothesized, they were the Big Bosses. The freaks had to answer to them! "Oh, we started out as performers," said Papa Catface, "but a little business sense changed that in a hurry." He chuckled and the children gathered about him at his feet.

Catface asked, "Where's Maria?"

His mother answered, "Oh, she's out and about. She'll be back soon."

Mama Catface turned to Christine and me and she said, "Maria is Gerard's twin sister."

A twin sister! My God, the secrets old Catface had kept from me. And he had been upset over my not telling him about Christine's puppies. "I'd like to meet Maria," I said.

"Oh, she'd like you," said Mama Catface, and I was glad to hear that.

Then a normal-faced young man walked in and he went over to whisper something in Papa Catface's ear. Papa Catface nodded and said, "Send him in."

The young man left and Papa Catface said to us, "Someone has come with a business proposition."

There was a bustling about outside. I heard the familiar yips of young canines and then that horrible high-pitched whine of a voice which could only come from the man we all knew as Thurber. He burst into the tent with a bulging burlap sack slung over his shoulder. His skinny body was covered in dust and grime.

"Get away from me!" he was saying, "I don't need your Goddamn help!"

Thurber plunked the squirming sack down on the

floor. He looked up and saw big Papa Catface first, then Catface, and then me.

"Hello, Thurber," I said.

"What the hell are you doing here?" he said to me.

Christine rushed forward and opened up Thurber's sack. The little puppies came spilling out, squealing with delight and joy. She said, "Oh, my little darlings," and they jumped upon her, licking at her face.

Catface stood up and walked toward Thurber.

"Well, hello, Catface," said Thurber.

"My name is Gerard," said Catface.

"What's going on here?" said Thurber. His dirty face was filled with anger and confusion.

"You stole these puppies," said Catface.

"I did not," said Thurber. "I bought them off a merchant on the street."

Catface said, "Get out," and Thurber stood there for a moment trying to think of something else to say. His weasel-like eyes darted around the room. I could see him trying to take it all in. Poor Thurber. He must have thought he'd hit upon a gold mine with those mutant puppies, and now this.

Finally Thurber said, "Forget it," and he left the tent.

Catface knelt down and he nestled his face into the mass of puppy bodies. They licked at him and he said, "Oh, what lovely creatures."

We all sat and watched as Catface let the puppies

crawl over him. He laughed like a child and spoke to them in a crazy little voice. "Oh, what nice puppies," he chirped. "Oh, what wonderful little puppies." That voice! It was Squeak the rabbit! But I did not tell him so.

The Catfaces invited us to stay for dinner, a scrumptious feast of rice and beans. We ate it up as the mutant pups played around our feet. When the meal began to wind down Catface took Christine by the hand and he said, "Let's go for a walk."

I was left alone with the family of catfaces and in the awkward silence which followed the woman known as Maria walked in. She had shiny golden hair and a face just like a cat.

Mama Catface introduced us. She said, "Maria, I'd like you to meet a friend of Gerard's." We shook hands.

Then Maria smiled at me and she said, "Would you like to come with me and see the fairgrounds?"

And I said, "Yes, I would."

Mollusks

M y friend Kenneth and I were looking through some old automobiles we had found out in a field. We thought maybe there was something valuable in them. One time Kenneth found an old radar gun in a similar situation, the kind cops use to check a car's speed. It didn't work, but he kept it for parts.

These cars out in the field seemed like they had once been on fire. The paint was all bubbly and peeled. There were plants and other vegetation growing up practically through the floorboards. Under the seat of an old Ford I found myself a silver cup. Solid silver, imagine that.

Kenneth crawled inside a green Pontiac which was set apart from the rest of them. He'd been in there not even a minute when I heard him yelling for me to come over. I took my time and he kept yelling, "Hurry up! Hurry up, you gotta see this . . ."

So I made my way around to the passenger-side door where I could see Kenneth gazing at something he'd found in the glove compartment. I peered inside too and what a sight it was. Right there in that glove box sat a quivering yellow slug about the size of a large loaf of bread.

Kenneth and I watched it for a while, just to see it move. Its skin was all glistening, covered with slime.

"Jesus Christ," said Kenneth.

So we decided to take the giant slug home with us. Actually, it was Kenneth's idea. He said, "I know what we're gonna do. We're taking this puppy home."

I wouldn't necessarily have thought of it that way but then it's Kenneth who has the business sense. He is several years older than I am and he used to make his living doing this sort of thing. We found ourselves a big plastic bag, the kind they give you at the supermarket, and I held it open while Kenneth rolled the slug over. It just fell in there, *plop*. That slug was heavy, like a big ham, a little softer maybe.

Here's what we had scavenged in just about fifteen minutes at that place: a silver cup (solid silver, mine), an old Zippo lighter (broken, Kenneth's), and a giant slug (maybe ten pounds, Kenneth's, mostly).

I held the slug on my lap on the drive back. Kenneth wanted me to be very careful with it. "Don't break its skin," he kept saying. "Don't let any salt get on it." Right. Where was I going to find salt?

We went straight to Kenneth's house. He lives in a nice place but it's all trashed since he and his crazy wife, Terresa, never throw anything away. I heard Kenneth say this once, he said, "It costs ten dollars a month to have them fuckers come over here and haul away the garbage. Why should I pay that? Give me one good reason."

Kenneth was particularly excited at the prospect of showing the slug to Terresa. He was so excited that he screeched into the driveway and knocked over some plastic milk crates full of trash. "Whoops," he said, and then he hopped out of the car.

"Terresa, baby, you got to COME QUICK! You got to come out here and see this! You got to see what we found today!" he yelled.

Out walked Terresa and her eyes were all wide like she couldn't wait to see what we had in store for her. Terresa was very small, childsize almost. She and Kenneth made a funny couple, what with him being so uncommonly stout. I don't know what Terresa thought we had in that plastic bag, but it sure wasn't a big yellow slug.

She screamed and then went over to Kenneth and kicked him in the shin. She said, "What the fuck did you bring that here for?"

Kenneth was busy holding his aching shin so I piped up, "We figure someone will pay us for it."

"Yeah, right," said Terresa. She put her little hands on her hips. "That thing is disgusting."

I began to feel embarrassed. Oh, God, I thought. Just look at me. What a fool. After all, I was the one holding the bag. I must have looked like some sort of creep.

But Kenneth stuck to his guns. He said, "Disgusting does not mean undesirable."

Terresa didn't buy that. She whirled around and stomped back into the house. What a firebrand. See, I knew she was Kenneth's wife, but even so I liked her quite a lot. *"Thou shalt not covet they neighbor's wife,"* right? Well, fuck that, I thought, look at Kenneth. He collects slugs, giant ones. Where does he get off marrying a woman like Terresa?

We put the giant slug in one of Kenneth's old fish tanks. Actually, the tank still had fish in it, but Kenneth dumped them out to make room for the slug. He dumped them right on the floor of his garage where they flipped about on the cement.

"I'll show her," he kept saying. "I'll make a mint off this slug and then you and me will go off on a trip without her."

"Yeah, right," I said. But what I was really thinking was, This is my chance. I know, it was crass of me, but remember, Kenneth had just dumped a bunch of helpless fish onto the ground. Where was the compassion in that?

So, while Kenneth was tending to the slug, I went inside and found Terresa. She was at her loom, weaving. She had an enormous loom in the house. It took up a whole room and there was string and yarn everywhere. She made rugs with it.

I said to Terresa, "Hey, I've got a surprise for you."

She said, "It better not be another fucking mollusk."

"No," I said, "it's a cup, solid silver."

I held out the cup I had found and Terresa stopped working. She had this way of raising just one eyebrow. It was a very sexy thing to do. She said, "Are you sure you want to give that to me?"

I wasn't making much money then. I worked three nights a week at the Texas School for the Blind chasing after the children and putting them to bed after supper. It didn't pay very well. Terresa was right: I needed everything I got, even that little cup. So I said to her, "Oh, maybe I *should* hold on to it," and she nodded knowingly. What a vixen.

Then Kenneth walked in, saying, "I've got some phone calls to make."

It turned into night. Outside it grew dark and for hours and hours Kenneth kept at it on the phone.

"Yeah, Leroy," he would say, "I've got something very unusual here. I think you're gonna like this. . . . Yeah, right. . . . We found it this afternoon. . . . It's a giant slug . . . over ten pounds, easy. . . . What? . . . Oh, come on, Leroy. . . . Leroy? . . . Fuck." And then he'd try someone else.

Meanwhile, I was doing my best with Terresa.

"That's a nice rug you're making," I said.

"Thank you," she said. Her childlike hands scampered up and down the vertical strings. The rug was made of many colors, bright yellows and blazing reds. The truth is it was very ugly. I would have gotten sick having something like that on my floor.

Kenneth: "Hi, Mr. Logan. . . . Yes, Bob Willis referred me to you. . . . Right, he said your organization might be interested in a scientific find I've come across . . ."

"I'm sorry about the slug," I said to Terresa.

She said, "Oh, that's okay. I'm used to Ken's bullshit by now."

Bullshit! I thought to myself, She's dissatisfied!

Kenneth yelled over the phone, "Oh, Jesus! That's awful! You people ought to be gassed!" He slammed down the receiver and came running over to us.

"Those Satanists wanted to *burn* the slug!" he said, "They've got some kind of voodoo ritual involving mollusks! Isn't that fucked?" Kenneth looked tired. He'd been pulling his greasy hair this way and that.

"I think you're getting too attached to that thing, honey," said Terresa.

"Yeah," I said. "How much were they going to pay you?"

Kenneth looked shocked. He spun around and stormed off in a huff. "You Nazis!" he called out. "Fucking sellouts!"

Terresa turned to me and she said, "Can you and me go and talk somewhere private?"

I said, "Sure." All I could think was, Now's my chance, now's my chance.

There was nowhere to move in that trash-filled house so we ended up in the garage. There was that giant slug, sitting in the fish tank, all lit up and glowing yellow.

What a monster! It was too big for the tank. Part of its slimy tail slapped up against the glass.

"I sure hope that thing doesn't escape," I said.

Terresa looked up at me with solemn eyes and she said, "I haven't told Kenneth about this yet. I haven't told anybody. I'm with child."

"Oh, hey," I said, "a baby."

Terresa began to cry and I took her into my arms. I put my hand on her stomach. "Where's the kid?" I asked her. I couldn't feel it.

"It's not big enough yet," she said.

"Okay," I said.

We stood there holding each other in that strange aquarium light. I took my hand off of Terresa's stomach and motioned toward the quivering slug. "Maybe your baby will come out like that," I said. I'd intended it as some sort of joke, but Terresa didn't take it like that.

"Oh, God," she said.

I moved a little closer and under my foot I felt the body of one of those dead fishes go *squish*. It wasn't very romantic, but I leaned down and kissed her all the same.

Terresa didn't push me away, but she didn't seem very turned on, either. Her lips were cold. I stopped kissing her. I hugged her tight and pulled her little body close to mine. I whispered in her ear, "I can take you away from all this, Terresa. I can take care of you."

Of course, I couldn't. I had always looked up to Kenneth. I don't know why I decided on that day that I was a better man for Terresa. But it didn't matter. Kenneth walked into the garage as we were hugging like that and he stood there shocked. He looked first at Terresa, and then at me, and then at Terresa again.

Then he looked at the slug. "Dammit," he said.

He went over to the garage door and heaved it open. The night air rushed in. Kenneth walked back to the tank and reached his hands inside. With a loud grunt he hoisted the beast up and over his head. He stood there holding it high, like a first-place trophy, or a prize fish, and he looked down at Terresa and me.

"I'll be damned," he said, "if I'm going to let this slug come between us."

Kenneth dashed out the garage door, slug in hands, and heaved it with all his strength into the night. It landed with a dull thud out on the lawn.

"I don't care how much they were going to pay me," he said, almost tearful.

I let go of Terresa and she rushed over to Kenneth and wrapped her arms around him. Kenneth wiped his hands on his pants, to get rid of the slime, and then he hugged her, too. I had to admit, things looked better that way.

The slug made its escape that night, leaving a thick trail of ooze which disappeared into the woods. Perhaps it found some other abandoned glove compartment to call home. I found out later that some collector had offered Kenneth five hundred dollars for that slug, so it wasn't an empty gesture, tossing the animal away like that. I was sad at first to hear about that money lost. I thought Kenneth was a fool. But then I thought, Who are we to decide the fate of the earth's creatures? Who are we to cast judgment? It was the mollusks, after all, who first inhabited this earth. They roamed the land for millions and millions of years before any of us were even born.

The Texas School for the Blind

I was given charge of an eleven-year-old boy named Marvin who was both blind and deaf. He would walk around with his head down and both his arms waving about in front of him so that he could feel if he was going to bump into anything. Sometimes he would just take off and run, zigzagging around the room until he got tripped up or smacked into some object which his outstretched hands did not detect.

I had no idea how to communicate with Marvin. During the day he attended classes with trained professionals who tried to teach him words by drawing letters onto his palm with their fingers. No one explained to me how this worked. My job was to get him some exercise, feed him dinner, and put him into bed.

I would often talk to Marvin, though I understood,

obviously, that he could not hear me. I'd say things like, "Look out, Marvin!" or "Come here."

An interesting thing about Marvin was that he could identify people by the way they smelled. Each afternoon, when I picked him up at the school building, he would take my arm and sniff it. When we walked together, with Marvin holding my arm lightly at the elbow like we'd been taught, he'd keep his head pointed down, like a hunchback. I tried to get him to hold his head up, but he didn't like that. It was understandable, I guess, why he would see no reason to hold his head up while he walked.

Marvin and I never really became good friends. He bit me the first time I tried to give him a shower. He didn't like water touching his skin. He would often grab my arms and squeeze very tightly and it was for this reason I made sure to keep his fingernails cut short. The residential staff had a set of fingernail clippers which we were supposed to use for such tasks, but Marvin had unusually thick fingernails and I couldn't get the clippers to fit around them. So I used a set of scissors from the office. They were very sharp scissors designed for cutting paper and they performed the job well.

One evening I was getting Marvin ready for bed and he grabbed my hair and wouldn't let go. When I finally pried his fingers loose I noticed that his nails needed to be cut. I got the scissors from the office and began to clip away. Then Marvin grabbed my hair again with his other hand. I put down the scissors and tried to pry him off. He was pretty strong. I sat there trying to break free for quite a while. I was thinking about picking up Marvin and dunking him into a tub of water so that he'd be forced to either drown or let me go. Then I noticed that there were streaks of red blood on the bedsheets and suddenly there was a warm damp spot underneath where I was sitting. I thought, "Marvin has cut me."

But what had actually happened was he had grabbed the scissors with his other hand, the hand which wasn't holding my hair, and stabbed himself in the leg. This was a real mess. I'm not even sure if Marvin knew what he had done. I picked him up and wrapped him in the sheet. I ran down the hallway with Marvin in my arms. He was still holding on to my hair. When we reached the front desk I got on the phone and dialed for an ambulance. As we waited, I tried again to pry my hair from his fingers. Eventually I saw that he would never release me so I just tugged it hard and he took a whole fistful of my hair with him. Then I sat him on a plastic chair and used towels to soak up the blood, which was dark and copious, from his leg. Then the ambulance arrived.

I expected Marvin to wrestle with the paramedics, but he was very calm. Perhaps he'd been through this before. Maybe he recognized them by the way that they smelled. The paramedics wrapped his leg up tight and off we went to the hospital. Marvin had punctured a large vein in his inner thigh. It wasn't an artery, they said, but close. They gave him fourteen stitches and a pint of new blood. When we got back from the hospital the supervisor at the school made me fill out several pages of "incident report" forms and then I had to clean up the bed. The mattress was coated with plastic to protect it from bed wetting, so I just rinsed it off in the shower. After I was through I met with the residential staff supervisor who explained that I should never have brought those scissors into his room. I should have filled out a request form for a more hefty pair of clippers.

I was suspended from work for two weeks while they reviewed my conduct. When I returned to the school I was no longer working with Marvin. I was transferred to another dormitory altogether. There I was given charge of two brothers from Mexico, Santos and Miguel. Their parents were farmworkers who had been exposed to some strong pesticides in South Texas. As a result Santos and Miguel had been born without eyes. Where their eyes should have been, they had these little flesh-colored balls of skin.

But Santos and Miguel could hear everything. Their ears worked well. They knew how to communicate. Everything with them would be fine.

South for the Winter

It was growing cold where I was living and I could see from the way the clouds were bunching up that snow would soon fall. I like snow just as much as anyone else, but that winter I made up my mind to try something different. I decided to head south.

I went to my friend Eric's place to see if I could borrow his car. Eric is blind and doesn't drive. He owns a car so that other people can drive him places.

"Hey, Eric," I said, "do you think I could borrow your car for a little while? I need to get out of town, see the countryside."

Eric said, "Listen, I'm tired of you disappearing with my car. I lent it to you two weeks ago and you were gone for days. Why don't you take a bus?"

I hadn't thought of taking the bus. "I don't have much money," I said to Eric. "Can you lend me some?"

Eric sighed. He was staring off into the distance with glassy eyes, the way blind people do. "Lend you some money," he said, "or give you some?"

"Both," I said.

Eric opened up his wallet and felt around inside it. He kept his money organized by a system of folds on the corner of each bill. Each denomination was grouped and folded in a special way. He said that in a pinch he could also tell how much money he was holding by feeling the shape of the ink on the paper. Eric pulled out nine dollars—a five and four ones—and handed them to me.

"Thanks, Eric," I said. I put the money in my pocket, fully intending to take a bus ride south. But as I turned to leave I noticed Eric's car keys hanging off a hook on the wall. I walked toward them, pretending that something else over there had caught my eye. Eric was looking right at me but, of course, he couldn't see what I was doing. I slipped his car keys off the hook, being very careful not to let them jingle.

I coughed and said good-bye to Eric. Then I walked around back to where his car was. I suppose Eric knew exactly what was up when I started the engine on his big red Ford. He probably recognized the sound right away. It also made a lot of noise as I pulled out onto the road, clattering and clunking about, but it was too late for Eric to stop me then. I was headed south.

Eric had no maps at all in his car, so I just looked for the highway signs that said SOUTH. The open road! Yes! I drove for two and a half hours and then I ran out of gas on the freeway. I had been so pleased to be moving along that I had foolishly neglected to look at the gas gauge. Now I was stuck on the side of the road and the tank was dry.

I tried for a while to flag down passing motorists, but they had no sympathy for my plight. Finally a police cruiser came along and stopped beside me. I explained to the officer that I no longer had any gas. Apparently the highway patrol makes a policy of carrying three-gallon jugs of gasoline in all of their vehicles for just this sort of situation. I thought this was a real stroke of luck until the cop asked to see my driver's license, which I didn't have. Since I don't own a car I never bothered to get one. I showed the cop the registration to Eric's car and told him that I was Eric, thinking that this would make things go smoother. This turned out to be a stupid thing to do, though, because when the cop entered Eric's name into his computer he discovered that Eric was blind.

"Are you blind?" asked the cop.

"No," I admitted, "I'm not."

So the cop radioed the station and had them call Eric's house. Eric was upset, which was understandable. He informed the authorities that I had stolen his vehicle.

"You stole from a blind man?" asked the cop.

"I borrowed it without his permission," I said.

I was taken back to the station and then escorted to a small cell. They searched me for illegal substances and made me remove my shoes and also my belt so that I wouldn't go and hang myself. I spent six hours in that cell before a thin-lipped constable came to speak with me.

"Just what did you think you were doing?" he asked.

"I was trying to get south for the winter," I explained.

"I see," said the constable. He looked me over and pursed his colorless lips. I was standing there holding on to my pants with one hand so that they wouldn't fall down.

"Your friend Eric just called us," said the constable. "He said he didn't want to press charges this time."

That was a nice thing for Eric to do, I thought—really nice, considering the circumstances.

"You can go now," said the constable. He inserted his key and opened the door to my cell. I walked past him and got my shoes and belt back from the front desk. I slid the belt through the loops in my pants and tightened it up. Then I slipped my feet into my old leather shoes and walked outside into the night.

It had begun to snow—huge, fat, white flakes descending from the black sky. I let them gather on my head and shoulders and watched them melt upon my upturned palms. They were enormous, the biggest snowflakes I had ever seen in my life. I could have built myself an igloo out of each one of them.

Mattress

I moved into the house after Phil checked himself into a hospital up in Dallas. Phil's absence, they said, made room for me, but the place was still pretty full. There were eight of us in there with only three bedrooms. We stuck our beds in the dining room, in a big closet, and down in the basement. I didn't own a bed so I slept on a thin foam camping pad on the floor. For two months I slept like this, and it wasn't that bad, but I kept my eye out for something better all the same.

Eventually I saw an ad in the newspaper. It said: "FOR SALE—mattress and box spring—$50—U pick up."

I called the woman who had placed the ad and told her I wanted that mattress and box spring. I arranged for one of my housemates, Blake, to help me pick them up. Blake owned a big black pickup truck. We left after dark.

I had written the woman's name and address on a piece of paper which I held in my hand as Blake sped his truck along the bumpy roads. She lived on a little dead end road on the south end of town and I had to strain my eyes in order to see the street signs through Blake's dirty windshield.

"Slow down," I said to him. "I think we passed it."

But Blake did not slow down. Instead he whirled the truck around in a deft skid so that soon we were speeding along equally fast in the opposite direction. We raced around those narrow streets for close to a half hour before we finally ended up where we needed to be. We'd passed her road several times on the fly, but I never saw the sign far enough in advance to warn Blake about it.

Blake slid to a stop in front of the house. We both got out and slammed our doors hard. I was glad to be free of that crazy vehicle.

"You drive like Mario Andretti," I told Blake.

"I don't know him," he said.

"He drives racecars," I said.

"Oh, yeah. Gotcha. Ten-four." Blake hopped up on the doorstep and began rapping away on the door. He kept knocking on it until the woman came out. She stared blankly at him from behind the screen.

"We're here about the bed," said Blake.

"Okay, yeah," said the woman.

She opened the door and let us in. Her feet were bare and she wore only a terry cloth robe. I wondered if she was naked beneath it. As she walked ahead of us I took note of her nice, rounded calf muscles. She had been very curt and to the point on the phone, leading me to expect someone much older. But this person here was twenty-four, perhaps twenty-five, years old, just a little older than myself.

She led us upstairs to a loftlike bedroom where a queen-size bed sat on the floor. There was no frame, just the mattress on top of the box spring, a simple setup which I admired. The sheets and blankets were still on the bed, strewn about as if she had been lying there just moments before.

"Here's your bed," she said.

Blake and I looked around the room stupidly, thinking there must be some other bed in there.

"You can lie on it first if you want," said the woman. She made a motion toward the unmade bed. It was indeed the one which was for sale.

I lay down on it just to satisfy her. I planned to take the mattress and box spring regardless of what they felt like. The price was good, and I was tired of sleeping on the floor. I thought I detected a trace of warmth lingering in the sheets, but that could have been my imagination.

I said to the woman, "I hope you're not selling me your only bed."

"Oh, I am," she said. She drew a half circle on the floor with the toe of her bare foot. "I'd just like to get rid of that thing, you know?"

Blake asked, "Is there something wrong with it?"

"There's something wrong with it for me," she said.

Blake gave her a sort of knowing smile. He was doing some kind of creepy impression. Most likely he saw himself as coming across coy and mysterious. The woman clutched her robe a little tighter and turned away from him. It was the right thing to do when Blake got like that. She looked at me, sitting there on the bed.

"It feels okay to me," I said. "I'll take it."

"Great," she said. "You can put those sheets and blankets in the corner."

She turned to go downstairs but Blake tapped her lightly on the arm. Still grinning, he asked her, "Where are you going to sleep tonight?"

"On the couch," said the woman.

I began removing the sheets, hoping that Blake would join in and leave her alone. He stood there regarding the woman for just a moment longer, then closed his eyes and bowed, letting her pass.

We hauled the mattress down first. It was shiny and new, still bearing that strange label which said, "DO NOT REMOVE THIS TAG UNDER PENALTY OF LAW." What a deal I had struck up. Fifty dollars!

The box spring was more difficult to maneuver down the stairs. Several times we bumped into the walls and left little chips and dents in the paint. Blake would curse when this happened, spitting out vile expletives which made me uneasy since we were in the home of a stranger. The woman remained stoic in front of her television set, though. She didn't even get up to say good-bye.

We loaded the box spring into the truck first. Then we tossed the mattress on top, jumped into the truck, and drove away.

DOGWALKER

Once we'd made it out onto the main road Blake
fished out a half-smoked cigarette from his ashtray. He
lit it up with the truck's lighter, pressing the blackened
end onto the glowing orange coils. Then he took a long
drag. He let it out and said, "That girl's got LeAnne's
eyes."

This was an ongoing saga for Blake. Every new
encounter, every offbeat conversation, somehow brought
to his mind the image of this woman LeAnne. She had
been his girlfriend back in his hometown. A few years
ago they had conceived a child together and sometime
after that Blake left town. The child was a boy. Blake
kept a picture of him, one of those drugstore photo por-
traits, on display in our kitchen. He was a smiling little
tot, with short-cropped hair and a set of dark, confused
eyes. Blake would point to the picture and say, "That's
my boy."

I tried not to react to the LeAnne remark. I didn't
want to start all that going again.

"Why do you think that girl was selling her bed?" I
asked him.

"Now, see, that's what I was trying to figure out."
Blake became excited, chopping his hands through the
air for emphasis, hardly keeping his eyes on the road at
all. "The way I see it," he said, "something real bad
happened to her on that bed." Blake smiled. He fancied
himself an acute observer of the human condition.

"Maybe she just needs the money," I said.

"No, no. It ain't that," said Blake. "Beds are very personal."

I thought about that and decided it was true. I felt funny taking something from someone which was so meaningful. Would I be able to rest easy knowing this bed was the host to so many hours of solitude, private intimacies, and dreams?

"What do you think happened to her?" I asked Blake.

"Oh, it could be any number of things. Nightmares, fights of passion, lost love. LeAnne did the same type of shit. She wanted me to take back everything I ever gave her. She probably sold her damn bed, too."

"I see," I said.

I had never met LeAnne, but I felt sorry for her all the same. The vengeance heaped upon her! Blake used to call her up on the phone late at night and not say a word. He'd just stare at the receiver in his hand. Later on, she would call back and scream so loudly that we could hear her muffled voice from the other room. I couldn't feel too bad for her, though. Blake tended to attract women who were looking for the "dangerous type" of guy, and I figured LeAnne must have at one time been looking for this as well.

We crossed the bridge which led us over Lake Austin. In reality this body of water was no lake. It was actually the Colorado River. It didn't have much flow to it around here though and I had to admit it looked more like a lake. Blake was from a town a little ways north of here called Lake Watson. I once asked him about the actual lake his town had been named after. I wanted to know if he went fishing there as a small child. Blake gave me a curious look and said that, in point of fact, there was no lake at all in Lake Watson.

"There was a pond. It was called Denton Pond, and I used to spear bullfrogs there," he said wistfully.

We were cruising along at a ridiculous pace. On Guadeloupe Avenue, where there was a long succession of traffic lights, Blake roared ahead and stopped at each red light just before it turned green. I suppose it never occurred to him to slow down and time the lights correctly so as to avoid all that jerking around.

Blake said, "You know, the night my boy was born I drank a whole bottle of Jack Daniels. I downed the whole thing myself."

I couldn't tell if this was a lie or not. Blake liked his wild-guy image, and he often stretched the truth for the sake of a story. But then again, this also rang out as some sort of confession. I imagined Blake, shit-faced and alone, while his child took his first screaming breaths of air.

I said to him, "That's a lot of whiskey."

"Sure is," said Blake. He ground the truck into second gear as he slowed down to make a turn. "She wouldn't let me see my boy for two months after he was born. She let my own mother at him before me."

"That must have been rough," I said.

"When I did get to see him I could tell that he possessed genius. My boy's got the eyes." Blake tapped the side of his forehead with his index finger. "Genius," he said again.

We jerked to a stop in front of our big house. Blake and I got out of the truck and went around back to get the bed. The mattress was gone. The box spring remained but the mattress was nowhere in sight. It had flown up into the air during the ride and landed on the road without us even noticing. What fools! My mattress, abandoned on some dirty roadside!

"I can't believe it," I said, although it did make sense. All that speeding around and we hadn't even bothered to tie it down.

"Man," said Blake, "that's the first time I ever lost a load. I've never lost a load." He said this with such conviction that I believed him, even though, in retrospect, it seems pretty unlikely.

"If we go back and retrace our steps we could probably find it," I said.

Blake said, "Yeah, okay," but he was headed up toward the house.

"Where're you going?" I asked him.

"I need a beer first."

I followed him inside and into the kitchen where we came upon our housemates Kris and Valerie. They were wrapping dried-out animal bones in steel wire. The bones had been gathered from the desert, skulls and spinal cords, antlers, and the long teeth of the coyote.

Kris and Val were piecing them together into some kind of mosaic. The smell of marijuana smoke filled the kitchen. Laura the dancer was at the counter, cutting up vegetables.

"Where's the bed?" she asked me.

"We lost it," I said. "It fell out of Blake's truck."

Blake nodded his head in agreement and made his way over to the refrigerator to get his beer.

"We've still got the box spring, though," I said.

Blake said, "I've never lost a load before." He went over to the windowsill where Laura kept her pills and emptied a few of them into the palm of his hand.

Laura eyed him suspiciously. "I hope you haven't eaten anything," she said. "You're not supposed to eat anything before you take those."

"I haven't eaten all day," said Blake. It was probably true. I rarely saw Blake eat. Now that I think about it, I don't think I ever saw Blake sit down and eat a meal the whole time I lived there. He appeared to live on beer, cigarettes, and pills. Blake popped the little yellow tablets into his mouth and washed them down with a swig from his can of Old Milwaukee.

"I think you should call the police," said Laura. "Someone might have seen it on the road and reported it to them."

Blake hoisted himself up on the counter and sat down. "No cops," he said. "Don't call them. That's a bad idea."

I watched Kris and Val piece together their bone art.

They planned to hang it up on a wall. When it was done, said Kris, it would resemble some sort of prehistoric creature.

"That's looking pretty good," I said to them.

"Thanks," said Kris.

Nearly an hour passed before Blake or I made a move to go back out. It was easy to lose track of time in that kitchen. Sometimes I feel as if my whole year was spent sitting in that room, telling stories and laughing at our misfortunes. Eventually Blake got up and hit me on the shoulder. I got up, too.

"We're gonna go find that mattress," I said.

We went outside and took the box spring out of the truck, leaving it on the curb in front of the house. Then we got back in the truck and set off once again into the night. We did our best to retrace the exact route we took on the way home, but this was a difficult task given Blake's bandito driving style. At one point we boldly sped in the wrong direction down a one-way street. Oncoming headlights flashed ominously in our faces.

"This is wrong, Blake," I said.

Blake told me to relax and keep an eye out for that mattress. He had taken the task to heart. He kept repeating that line: "I never lost a load."

We crossed the bridge over Lake Austin and still we had not seen the missing mattress. "Maybe someone else found it," I suggested. "Maybe someone who really needs it, a mother with small children who has been sleeping on the cold floor . . ."

"That's ridiculous," said Blake. "More likely the cops got it. Or some furniture scavengers. They'll just sell it for profit, you know."

Furniture scavengers! I tried to imagine the actual quantity of useful furniture one could gather from the streets. It didn't seem like much.

Blake was humming some Texas tune, his head craning one way and then another in search of the lost load. I had grown tired of warning Blake to watch the road, but I wish I had kept it up just a little while longer. We came off the bridge and the truck drifted dangerously close to the curb. Blake took notice of this just in time, but his reaction was too strong. He whipped the truck away from the curb with a quick jerk of the wheel and sent us plowing head-on into a car parked on the opposite side of the road. The crushing sound of metal against metal was tremendous. Blake's big truck had buried its front end into one of the car's side doors. We sat there for a moment, touching our own faces with our hands, feeling to see if anything was broken.

"Motherfucker," said Blake. He put his truck in reverse and backed it away from the mess he had made. From that distance we looked upon the car we had hit. One of the windows was smashed and the rear side door was punched in, wrinkled up like tinfoil. Luckily, there was no one inside.

"You got it pretty good there," I said.

"Fuck," said Blake. "We're gonna have to leave this one here."

"What do you mean?" I asked him. Cars passed by us, the passengers staring wide-eyed at the calamity on the side of the road. "There are witnesses," I said. "We can't just leave."

Blake sighed, grappling with this logic. He said, "I ain't waiting for the cops. No way."

"Leave a note then," I said. "That's the right thing to do."

We found a pen somewhere on his cluttered dashboard and on a ratty piece of paper Blake wrote:

You have been hit by Blake Wilson. My telephone number is 562-3742. Call if you desire further info.

He showed the note to me for approval and I said it looked fine. Blake left the scrap of paper under one of the car's windshield wipers where it flapped about in the wind like a parking ticket. What a shock it would be to return to that! I hoped the person whose car we had hit was someone who deserved such an event. First an abandoned mattress and now this. I imagined Blake and myself as messengers of Fate, dealing out Karma in brazen doses to those who were in need.

We drove the rest of the way to the woman's house without saying a word. The mattress was nowhere in sight. Blake stopped in front of her place.

"We shouldn't have waited so long back at the house," I said. "We let it sit out there for too long."

"Yeah, well, it's gone," said Blake.

"Let's go ask that woman if she's seen it," I said. I thought maybe it had fallen out right as we had left. Perhaps the woman had seen this happen and retrieved it for us.

"You go ahead," said Blake. "I don't want to see that girl again."

I went up and knocked on her door. Inside the house it was dark except for the dim blue light from the television. The woman answered the door, clearly just awakened from her slumber.

"Oh, I'm sorry to wake you up," I said.

The woman squinted and frowned at me.

"We lost that mattress you sold me," I said. "It flew out of the truck."

"I'm sorry about that," said the woman.

"Have you seen it?" I asked her.

"No, I haven't," said the woman.

"Okay," I said. I was embarrassed. Why had I come to her?

"Can I ask you another question?" I said.

"Yes," she said. "Sure."

"Why did you want to get rid of that bed?"

"It smelled funny," she said. "I have a real sensitive nose."

"Oh," I said. "I had thought it was because of bad dreams."

"Yeah, that too," said the woman. "All of that."

I said good night and went back to the truck where Blake was waiting for me.

"She hasn't seen it," I said.

"Figures," said Blake.

We headed home, past the car we had dented, and over the bridge. We drove through the empty downtown and up Guadeloupe Avenue. When we reached our house Blake stopped the truck.

"Thanks for your help, Blake," I said.

Blake said, "Yeah, you know, I always am good to help a friend out."

This certainly was true of Blake. He had once driven all the way out to some highway in Kansas to pick up a stranded acquaintance. He said the same thing then before he left for that trip, about being one to help a friend out. It meant a lot to him to be thought of as someone who could be counted on. Now I wondered which one of us was more upset about that "lost load."

"I appreciate it, Blake."

Blake turned off the engine and said, "LeAnne's with another man. My boy is being raised by another man."

The engine sputtered to a stop. When it got quiet I said to him, "I think you should go back there. You should go see your kid. That's what I think."

"Yeah, that's what you think," said Blake. He got out of the truck and slammed the door, leaving me alone. I sat there for a while, enjoying the solitude.

Inside the house there was loud music and the bones had been forgotten. Kris and Valerie were dancing in the hallway. Laura sat at the table, molding something out of clay. Blake stood talking to Aaron, our neighbor from next door. On the counter beside them lay a big plastic bag filled with wet mushrooms. There looked to be about a pound of them.

"Aaron went out to the hills and picked them this morning," said Laura. "Kris and Val ate some. They're good!"

Blake sipped away at his beer and I saw him flip one of the mushrooms into his mouth. I wandered into my room where someone had dragged my lone box spring inside and placed it in the corner. I flopped my body upon it and fell asleep. It wasn't so bad, sleeping on just the box spring like that. Later on I put my foam camping pad on top of it and that served as my bed for the rest of the year.

The House of
Alan Matthews

I went to see my friend Alan Matthews the other night. He is not really my friend but rather an acquaintance who I know usually has marijuana ready to sell. Alan lives in a cramped top-floor apartment over on Union Street. It used to be an attic and the ceilings are all crazy and angled like the shape of the roof. My plan in going there was to sit around for a while, smoke whatever he had to offer, then pick up a bag for myself and leave.

Alan answered the door wearing one of those white sleeveless undershirts. His eyes were little slits. Perhaps I had just woken him up. "Sorry to bother you," I said.

"Oh, no, hey," he said. "No problem. No problem."

Alan is older than me by a few years. He's settled into this weed-dealing lifestyle, I guess. He hangs around all day and waits for people to come over.

I took a seat on the floor and began staring up at the ceiling. There was hardly any room at all to stand up in there. Luckily for Alan, he was short. It gave him a little extra space.

"So listen, Alan," I said. "I heard something about you having some hash."

"Yes," he said, "that's true."

Alan was pacing about in a slow circle.

"Perhaps we could smoke some of that," I ventured.

"Sure, yeah, no problem."

Alan went over to a table in the corner and he pulled open a drawer. Inside the drawer were several plastic bags full of different varieties of pot. This was his personal stash.

We smoked the hash from his long red water pipe and Alan put a record on his turntable. It was some kind of Middle Eastern chant music with lots of wiry string sounds.

"Okay," said Alan, "how are you feeling now?"

"Just fine," I said, and I was.

Then I began to hear a thumping noise from behind the wall. At first I dismissed it as some sort of sensation brought on by the potency of Alan's hash, but the thumping grew louder and I could no longer put it out of my mind.

"What's that noise?" I asked Alan.

Alan was staring at one of his record covers. He didn't look up at me. He just said, "Yeah, don't worry about that."

The thumping grew louder still. It sounded like someone was knocking on the wall from the other side. "You got neighbors or something?" I asked. "Maybe you should turn that music down."

"Nah. No, it isn't that," said Alan. He cast a cool look my way. "He's not my neighbor."

"Okay," I said, and I tried to figure out what that was supposed to mean. There was an urgency in the knocking which made me uneasy. I scanned the wooden walls of Alan's little apartment and discovered a small door which I hadn't noticed on my earlier visits. It was only a few feet high, like the entrance to some kind of crawl space. I could see now that this was where the thumping was coming from.

Alan caught me staring at the wooden door.

"What's going on here?" I asked him.

"Here?"

"Yeah."

"Well, see," said Alan, "that's Ricardo there behind the door and he's banging on it because I won't let him out."

I tried to imagine the amount of space Ricardo had back there and it didn't seem like much.

"How long has he been in that closet?" I asked.

"Oh, yeah, quite a while," said Alan. "He'd like to go, probably."

Alan got up and went over to the corner of the room which was his kitchen. It was just a sink and a hot plate set on the counter.

"You want some tea?" he asked me.

"No thanks," I said. And then I added, "Maybe Ricardo wants some."

"Not likely," said Alan. "Why don't you ask him?"

So I did. I crawled over to the little door and I put my head up close to it. "Hey, Ricardo," I said, "you want some tea?"

The thumping stopped. There no reply so I repeated the question, "Hey, Ricardo, do you want some tea?"

I could hear Ricardo repositioning himself. I figured Alan must have tied him up in there. Eventually a voice came out from behind the door, "Did you just say, 'Do you want some tea?' "

"Yes," I said. I looked over at Alan who was paying no attention to us at all. He was washing dishes.

Ricardo was breathing heavily. I could hear it. All that bumping about must have tired him. "Okay," he finally said, "I'll take some of that tea."

"Great," I said. I called out to Alan, "Hey, Ricardo wants some tea."

Alan said, "Tell him 'fuck you.'"

"Oh," I said.

I leaned a little closer to the door. "Did you hear that?"

"What?" said Ricardo.

"Alan said you can't have any."

There was a tremendous clattering. Ricardo must have been thrashing about with all his might. The little door was well made though, and it held fast. Alan heard the clamor and he yelled out, "Okay! Hey! Would you knock it off?"

"He's mad because you won't give him some tea," I said.

"He's mad because I won't let him out of that closet."

Alan and I watched the door shake and rattle about until the thumping finally died down. Alan sipped at his tea.

"There," he said to Ricardo. "Aren't you glad you went through all that trouble?"

We could hear Ricardo taking deep, heaving breaths. Every so often he would cough.

"When are you going to let him out?" I asked Alan.

Alan sucked the steam off the surface of his tea. "Hard to say," he said.

"Okay," I said, "then how about selling me some of that hash?"

"Sure," said Alan.

Alan sold me a few grams of hash, which didn't last me long because my friends soon found out about it and they all came by asking for handouts.

I said to them, "Why don't you just head over to Alan's and get it yourself?"

But they each said the same thing about Alan being too strange and weird these days. Nobody wanted to go over there. And who could blame them?

I went back myself a few days later. Things seemed

okay. Alan played his freaky records on the turntable and we got high on some strong Moroccan weed which smelled like apples. The little closet was empty and Ricardo was gone. Alan had let him out a while back. He had grown tired of all the thrashing and banging about.

"That guy was a real whiner," Alan said with a laugh.

Six Dog Christmas

Troy showed up at my house around Thanksgiving with a small purple duffel bag in his hands. There was something inside it, a heavy-looking lump about the size of a large potato.

"Here," he said to me. "Do you think you could hold on to this for a little while?"

"What is it?" I asked. I thought it must be something illegal, like a gun.

"It's one of the puppies," said Troy.

"Which one?"

"The yellow one, with the spot on its head."

Troy's mother's dog had given birth to a litter of puppies a few weeks ago. He was in charge of taking care of them. He pushed the bag at me. "Maybe you could put it in your fridge," he said.

"Is it dead?" I asked him. I'd seen the puppy the day before and it looked fine to me then.

"The radio fell on top of him," said Troy. "He couldn't walk and then he died."

"The radio?" I said.

"Right," said Troy.

I took the bag from Troy. He turned around and went back to his house down the street.

The puppy was dead all right. I left him in the bag and put it on the bottom shelf of my refrigerator.

Troy was seventeen years old. He wasn't allowed to go to school that year because he hadn't gotten his shots. That's what he said. He lived with his mother in a little house they shared with a roommate. I never saw the roommate. Troy and his mother slept in the kitchen on a big dusty double bed. They had one of those mini-refrigerators, like you would see in a hotel room. Troy said that it was too small to hold the puppy.

The next day I spotted Troy smoking a cigarette by the bus stop.

"When are you going to get that puppy?" I asked him. "I can't keep it forever."

"I'll come by this afternoon," he said. Then the bus arrived and he got on it.

Troy didn't come by that afternoon, or the next day, either. I decided to go and see him, but no one answered when I knocked on the door. I went inside. The kitchen was crowded with dogs and they barked and jumped up on me. There were about ten of them in there. Most of them were puppies from the litter but a few came from somewhere else. Those were fully grown. The dogs ran all over the bed that Troy and his mother shared. I looked around for the radio that had fallen and killed the yellow puppy, but I didn't see it anywhere.

I went home and took the dead puppy out of my refrigerator. I dug a hole in my backyard and buried him there.

Troy came over several days later. It was nighttime and he had a friend with him, an older guy named Cliff.

"Where's the pup?" asked Troy.

"I buried him," I said. "I couldn't keep him forever."

Troy looked a little angry. He said, "Why'd you do that? I said I would come and get him."

"I didn't want to see it anymore." I said. "I keep food in my fridge."

Cliff stepped forward and tried to hit me. He was drunk and moved like a stiff old man. He stumbled and knocked over a table. Troy pushed over a lamp and tossed a book across the room. Cliff tried to turn over my sofa, but it was too heavy for him. Troy grabbed him by the coat and tugged him out the door.

On Christmas Eve I went to see Troy but only his mother was home. The puppies were much bigger now, nearly full-grown.

"Troy went out," Troy's mom said to me. "I need to go find him."

She got up and left me there alone with the dogs. The puppies tried to follow her but she kicked at them and shut the door behind her.

For a while, I just stood there in the kitchen and watched the puppies scramble about on the floor. They liked to chew and nip at one another's ears. I made up my mind right then to take them all home with me. Two by two I carried the puppies over to my house, one under each arm. There were six of them in all. Back at home, I fed them cans of ravioli and also some cereal with milk.

When I woke up in the morning there was snow on the ground, the first snow of the year. I took the puppies outside and they jumped around in it. Later on Troy showed up and asked me what I was doing with all of his puppies.

"I took them," I said.

"My mother wants to know where they are," he said.

"Tell her they got hit by radios," I said.

"That's not funny," said Troy. He was shivering in the cold. He didn't have any socks on. Little chunks of snow clung to his bare ankles and slid down the insides of his sneakers.

"I'll pay you for them," I said.

Troy bent down and scooped some snow out of his shoe with his finger. "I don't know about that," he said.

"I'll give you two dollars for each puppy," I said. "That's twelve dollars in all."

The puppies were rolling about on the ground behind me. They looked funny all covered in snow.

"You got twelve dollars on you right now?" asked Troy.

"I think so," I said. I went inside and found my wallet. There was exactly twelve dollars in it, two fives and two ones.

When I got back outside Troy was playing with the puppies in the snow. They bit his hands and tugged on his sleeves. Eventually he stood up and I handed him the money. He folded it up and put it in one of his pockets.

Troy shook his cold red finger at the dogs. "You stay here," he said to them. "Don't follow me home. Don't you follow me home."

And then he walked away down the street.

It was Christmas Day. I counted up my new dogs—one, two, three, four, five, six—and we all went inside where it was warm.

Bill McQuill

Bill was a large man with an apelike build. His arms were too long for the rest of his body. I said he was "large," but he wasn't actually that tall. If you saw him sitting down, and then he stood up, you'd be surprised at how short he really was. Those lanky arms just gave the impression of great height. Bill's face was kind of chunky and pockmarked, but he wasn't ugly. He was a sort of noble-looking person, as a matter of fact.

I'm not sure what else I can tell you about Bill by way of background. He and I both lived in an unusual old house over by the train tracks. We occupied separate apartments on the top floor. An older woman named Phylis owned the rest of the house and she rented out the two little places to us. Phylis was frail and rickety, just like the house. She rented the apartments to us very cheaply. They used to be her attic. To get inside we had to climb up a set of rusty metal steps which were actually designed as a fire escape, and then we had to crawl in through the bathroom window. Bill and I shared the bathroom. I always felt like a criminal creeping around like that, but as I said, Phylis rented out the place very cheap. Bill had been living there for almost two years before I moved in.

Bill liked to walk into my apartment unannounced. One time he walked in with a small pink bicycle in his hand. It was a tiny bicycle, a kid's bike, so he could carry it in just one hand. The wheels were about the size of pancakes.

"What do you think of this?" he said to me.

Bill placed the bike upon the table so that we could both look at it. There were little colored flowers printed on the white seat. Some of them were partially peeled off or faded from use.

"I don't see why you brought it over here," I said.

"I thought maybe you could use it. Didn't you say you needed a bicycle?"

This was Bill's idea of a joke. Earlier in the week, I had actually mentioned that I needed a bicycle. Of course, the one which Bill had brought over would not do. I went over to the window and looked outside. There was a young girl down there, wandering around the street. She was wearing dirty yellow pants and a hat. She walked around in an aimless circle. I watched her crouch down and peer underneath a bush.

"Did she see you take it?" I asked him.

"No."

"Well, I think you should give it back to her now."

"You sure you don't want it?"

"I don't want it."

"Okay, fine," said Bill, but he didn't make a move. He sat down in my chair and began to read one of his auto parts catalogs. Bill liked to hang out in my apartment for long periods of time, so I kept some reading material around for him. I wasn't a big fan of those catalogs myself.

The pink bicycle sat there on top of the table. It looked like a little statue. I couldn't believe anyone was small enough to ride something like that. I went over and picked it up.

"I'm going to give it back to her," I said.

"Knock yourself out," said Bill. This was one of his favorite phrases. He used it every chance he got. Anytime I suggested a particular course of action, especially one in which he did not want to participate, it was always, "Knock yourself out."

I carried the bicycle out the bathroom window and maneuvered with it down the fire escape stairs. When I got to the street the little girl was gone. I called out for her and checked under the bushes, but she had disappeared.

I left the bike on the sidewalk with a note on it. The note said something like, "Please leave this bike here for its proper owner."

For three days, through a heavy downpour even, that bike stayed where I'd left it. Then, one morning, it was gone.

———

Between the two of us, Bill was the better cook. He could actually prepare meals from scratch. Most of the food I had eaten prior to meeting up with Bill came from cans, or foil-covered packages. Bill actually enjoyed the whole process of slicing up vegetables and seasoning the meat. He would often invite me over to eat his homemade stew. He made some very good stews, I'll have to admit that. His apartment was always a mess. I usually had to move about six different piles of junk just to sit down. It smelled funny in there, too, like overripe fruit. One time I was eating his stew and I found a wristwatch floating in the sauce. It was just the watch part, without the band. Bill didn't believe in wearing watches, so I knew it wasn't his. When I picked up the watch with my fork Bill slapped his big floppy hands on his knees and bellowed with laughter. This incident is another example of Bill's unusual sense of humor.

As I mentioned before, the house where Bill and I lived was next to a set of train tracks. It was the Missouri-Pacific freight line. Bill was the one who introduced me to the pleasures of hanging out by the railroad. He liked to walk along the tracks and sit out there for hours on end. The rails stretched on for miles and miles in either direction and the unobscured views were very soothing.

The terrain around a set of high-voltage power lines can provide a similar feeling.

Every time a freight train passed by our house, the whole place would shake and rumble and the windows would rattle about in their frames. This was annoying to Bill, or at least I think it was. The walls of our apartments weren't very thick and I often overheard his personal commentary, things he thought he was saying just to himself. Right after a train went by he would shout out, "Fucking freight trains!" or "Goddamn trains!"

But if I ever asked him about this he would deny it. "Oh, I love trains," he would say to me.

One time Bill and I were walking along the tracks and we came upon two very badly injured dogs. They had both been hit by the train. One of them, a female, couldn't move its back legs. She just sort of scraped at the dirt with her front paws. The other one, a male, was pretty much dead. His side was all punched in and sticky with blood. The train had sliced off one of his feet, too. He was still breathing, though. I thought it was strange that two dogs would be so careless as to get hit by a freight train.

"They were probably having sex," said Bill. "Dogs get stuck together when they have sex."

"That would explain it," I said.

"I wish I had a shotgun," said Bill.

"So do I," I said.

Bill and I ran back to the house and knocked on Phylis's door. Bill thought she kept a gun around for protection. Phylis answered the door in her nightgown. It was about four o'clock in the afternoon.

"Do you have a shotgun, Phylis?" asked Bill. "We need to borrow your gun."

Phylis narrowed her eyes. "I'm not giving you my guns," she said. She was a very small woman. Bill and I towered above her.

"There's two dogs out on the tracks," I said. "We want to kill them."

Phylis drew in a quick breath and shut the door on our faces.

"That old witch," said Bill.

We went back to the tracks and found the dogs. The female had crawled off into the tall grass. Bill tried to pick her up but she bit him on the arm. Her back was broken, it was pretty easy to tell that.

"Shit," said Bill. "Fuck."

He went and found a big rock, one about the size of a bowling ball. He dropped it on the dog's head about four or five times.

"That should do it," said Bill.

Then he went and did the same thing to the male dog.

After he was done, I said, "I think we should bury them."

"Knock yourself out," said Bill.

He started walking back to the house and I couldn't face those dogs alone, so I left, too.

It was after that incident with the dogs that Bill began to really hate Phylis. Before that he seemed to have no strong opinion about her one way or another. He'd referred to her as "the crazy old lady" a few times, but that was about it. After the dog incident she became "Phylis the hag" or "Shotgun Phylis." I'd hear him muttering mean things about her through the walls at night.

Bill and Phylis had some sort of long-standing agreement whereby he would do things like take care of the yard and haul out her garbage in exchange for a reduced rent. Come to think of it, he may not have paid her any rent at all. Phylis would give him a list of chores at the beginning of each week and he would just go about doing them at his leisure. It seemed like a pretty good deal to me, but Bill began to really resent those notes from her. He claimed they'd changed in tone and now contained little hidden barbs about the quality of his work.

"Look at this," he told me one time. He handed me Phylis's note.

Among other things, the note said, "Please make sure all of the leaves get removed from the backyard."

"What does she expect?" hissed Bill. "I can't pick up

every Goddamn leaf that falls onto the grass. Who am I? Who does she think I am?"

At first I thought Bill was kidding about all this, but he wasn't. He was really upset. He continued to do his chores but at night his solitary tirades about Phylis's evil character became even louder and more involved. I had to purchase a set of earplugs just so I could sleep.

One morning I said to Bill, "You know, I think Phylis might be able to hear you through the floor. Maybe you shouldn't talk so loudly."

"What are you talking about?" said Bill. "I don't know what you're talking about."

"I think she might be able to hear the things you are saying in your room," I said.

"I don't say things in my room," said Bill.

Later on I realized that this was a stupid thing for me to bring up, because it just made Bill even more worried about Phylis and her supposed plots against him. He went out and bought a whole bunch of foam rubber padding and laid it down on his floors to insulate against sound transmission. Of course, he didn't bother to talk any softer.

It was around this time, I guess, that Bill came up with the notion of kidnapping Phylis. He came over to my place one afternoon all excited about the idea.

"We'll tie her up and keep her down in the basement," he said. "That way she can't bother us."

"She doesn't bother me," I said.

"You won't have to pay her any rent," said Bill.

"Someone will find out and we'll get arrested."

"She doesn't have any friends. No one would notice."

"I'm not going to do it," I said.

Bill said, "Okay, fine," and then walked out.

Once again, I couldn't tell if this was another one of Bill's mysterious jokes. Maybe he was just trying to get me in trouble. I could see him getting a big kick out of watching me try to tie poor Phylis to a chair. After I was done he'd slap me on the back and say something like, "Oh, I wasn't serious about this kidnapping business. Did you think I was serious?"

Although I wouldn't call Bill a hard-core drinker, he did have his moments of drunken excess. About once every month he'd purchase a bottle of Old Grand Dad whiskey ("a fine brand") and do his best to polish it off in one night. He was a pretty funny guy when he was drunk. He'd shout and dance around and then eventually he'd fall asleep sitting upright in a chair. I would occasionally drink with him, but he considered me a "wussy" because I liked to mix cola in with my whiskey.

One night Bill came over and invited me to his place for some stew and whiskey.

I said, "I'm going to get some cola first."

"Knock yourself out," said Bill. He went back inside his apartment.

I went out to get the soda, but when I came back I decided I didn't want to join him for that drink after all. I didn't like the way he had said "knock yourself out" that time. That phrase was getting on my nerves. Besides, I wasn't hungry for stew, and all Bill would want to talk about was Phylis. He had that old woman on the brain.

So I stayed home and read a book. I drank the cola straight, with a little ice. I couldn't tell if Bill had decided to drink the whiskey without me or not. He remained pretty quiet for most of the evening. I could hear muffled sounds, like he was having a quiet conversation. Maybe he found someone else to drink with, I thought, though it wasn't likely.

Before I went to sleep that night I did something I didn't normally do. I stuck my ear up against the wall so I could hear exactly what he was saying. He was talking in a very calm, relaxed voice.

"Was your laundry fluffy enough this morning, Phylis? Did I fluff it up enough for you? How about the lawn? I hope that met your high standards of satisfaction."

I put my earplugs in my ears and went to bed.

Throughout the next day the strange little banter continued.

"And what would you like for lunch, Miss Phylis?"

"Would you like me to open a window? Are you getting enough air?"

I went downstairs and knocked on Phylis's door. There was no one home. I went back upstairs and knocked on Bill's door. He answered it looking a little tired and strung out. He'd been drinking the whiskey.

"Is Phylis in there with you?" I asked him.

"Yes," said Bill, "as a matter of fact she is."

Bill opened the door and let me inside. Phylis was sitting on a small wooden chair facing the window. Her arms and legs were wrapped tightly to the chair with duct tape. Her mouth was taped shut as well. She had a somewhat calm expression on her face, though, as if all of this wasn't very surprising to her.

"Bill," I said, "this isn't a good idea."

Bill slapped me on the back and laughed. He stomped around the apartment coughing and sputtering between guffaws.

"That's a good one!" he chortled. "Oh, that's really good!"

I waited until he'd calmed down a little. Phylis just sat there breathing steadily through her nose, her eyes following Bill as he pranced about the room.

"Is this some kind of a joke?" I asked Phylis.

She shook her head, "No."

"Bill," I said, "how long has this been going on?"

"Did you bring your soda pop over?" said Bill. "You want to mix it with the whiskey?"

Bill held up his jug of Old Grand Dad. It was about half full.

"I drank my soda last night," I said.

"How about some stew? You want some stew?"

The stewpot was sitting on the table, on top of a pile of magazines.

"No, thanks," I said, "I don't need any stew."

"Wussy," said Bill.

"Where's your knife?" I asked. "I'm going to cut Phylis loose."

Bill walked over to a drawer and yanked it open. He rummaged through the utensils in there until he found his big knife. It was some kind of machete, actually, the kind of thing you might use to clear away brush in the jungle. Bill held it up and then he went over and stuck the tip of the blade into the table. It wouldn't stay upright, so he slammed it down again a little harder. The pot of stew bounced onto the floor and spilled everywhere. It was full of little metal parts—nuts and bolts, a bicycle chain, and small, pink child size pedals.

"I left a note on that bike," I said. "You were supposed to leave it there."

Bill nodded toward the machete. It had stayed stuck in the table this time.

"Knock yourself out," said Bill. He picked up his bottle of whiskey and walked out the door, leaving me alone with Phylis.

Phylis didn't say a word when I took the tape off her mouth. When I was through cutting her loose, she tried to stand up but her frail legs buckled beneath her and she fell to the floor. I tried to help her up, but she said, "Get your hands off me." She got up on her own and scurried down the stairs.

A few minutes later I heard gunshots and I looked out the window to see Phylis standing in the middle of the street with a big shotgun in her arms. She was just firing into the air. Bill was nowhere in sight.

The police arrived shortly after that and they asked me a few questions. I told them pretty much the same thing I've told you right here. I said I didn't know where Bill had gone off to.

Two days later, Bill came knocking on my door. It was very late at night and I had been asleep.

"What do you want, Bill?" I said.

"I can't get in my apartment," Bill said. "Phylis locked me out."

"If she saw you here she'd try to shoot you."

"Fuck her then."

"She's just an old woman."

"Yeah, right. I need to borrow some money. Can I borrow a few bucks from you?"

"I don't have very much."

"All I need is three dollars, that's all."

"Your breath stinks."

"Do you have three dollars?"

"I think I do."

"I'll pay you back."

"All I have is a five. Do you have change for a five?"

"No, of course not."

"Well, all I have is a five."

"Give it to me. I'll pay you back."

"I hope so."

I don't think I slept very well after he left that night. I was probably only half asleep, and that's why I noticed the sound the train made. It was about five a.m. It was still dark out, but it was beginning to get lighter. The train was rolling along, blowing its whistle, and then there was this loud cracking noise. Things started to hiss and pop and grind together. The windows of the house began to really shake. This went on for a while and then it stopped.

I heard men's voices, people yelling, so I got out of bed and put on some shoes. I climbed down the fire escape and walked out into the street. I walked past the trees, into the little meadow which ran alongside the tracks. The freight train was standing still, hissing, like a giant animal. Its wheels were as high as my chin. People were rushing around outside the train, yelling to one another and swinging flashlights around. I moved up close to them.

Someone yelled, "He's over here!"

I went over to where they were calling from and saw Bill McQuill lying on the tracks. Someone shined a flashlight on his face. Bill was talking to them. He was smiling and even laughing a little, so at first I thought he was okay. But then I saw that he was not.

The train had run Bill over just below the waist, cutting him in two. It was strange actually, because one of the wheels was still on top of him. His legs and feet must have been over on the other side.

"Hey," said Bill when he saw me. "This is a hell of a place to be, isn't it?"

"What happened, Bill?" I asked. I knew it was a stupid question, but I couldn't think of what else to say.

"I guess I fell asleep," said Bill. "I sure didn't expect this."

There wasn't much blood, really. The train's wheel was fit up snug against Bill's torso. It was holding things together.

"Somebody's calling an ambulance," I said. "They have a radio on the train."

"I can't feel a thing," said Bill. "Can you see my legs?"

I knelt down and looked into the darkness beneath the train. I couldn't see anything so I lied to Bill.

"Yes, I see them," I said.

"Tell them to bring those with me to the hospital," said Bill. "They can sew them back on."

"Okay," I said, "I'll tell them."

Blood was starting to trickle out from the corner of Bill's mouth. I felt pretty certain that he would die. I reached out to touch him, to maybe hold one of his big hands or something, but then someone yelled, "No!"

A team of paramedics arrived and surrounded him. They had bags of ice and tanks full of oxygen. "You're going to be okay," one of them said.

"No, I'm not," said Bill.

"We're going to move the train off of you."

"I'll lose all of my guts," said Bill.

"Not if we can help it."

"My guts will fall out."

"No they won't. It doesn't work like that."

"How the hell do you know?"

"I'm going to give you a shot now, for the pain."

"I can't feel anything anyway."

"Just try to relax."

They had hauled in a set of very bright lights. Suddenly it was as light as day, even lighter. A policeman grabbed my arm and started to pull me away.

"No," Bill said. "He's my friend."

They let me stay, but only if I stood over in a particular spot, away from the action. Everything had to be done very carefully. They couldn't move the train off of Bill until everything was set up just right.

I stood there in my assigned spot and tried to see what they were doing to Bill. The paramedics seemed very calm and collected. They kept telling Bill not to worry.

Something underneath the train kicked out at my foot. I jumped in the air. "Who was that?" I said.

I heard something pushing the gravel around so I crouched down and looked under the train. I saw Bill's legs. They were about thirty feet from where his upper body was. The train must have dragged them. Now the legs had started kicking around on their own.

I said, "His legs are over here!"

Nobody was listening to me. They were all too busy with Bill's upper half.

I decided to try to pull the legs out from under the train myself. They were really kicking around, though. They moved independently, bumping into the wheels and flicking gravel everywhere. Anyone who has ever seen the legs of an insect separated from the body will know what I mean here. The muscles just keep going on their own.

Eventually I managed to grab hold of one of Bill's feet. He had been wearing big work boots. It was hard to hold on. I got two hands on the boot and gave it a yank. It was hard to pull that leg out of there. You would have thought it was still attached to the rest of the body. When I got the leg out from under the train I tried to pick it up and carry it in my arms, but this turned out to be almost impossible. Bill's leg squirmed about like a big fish so I dropped it.

A cop saw me and ran over.

"What the hell are you doing?" he said.

"I've got one of his legs here," I said. "The other one's still under the train."

The cop shined his flashlight under the train and located the other leg. He went and grabbed it. He put the leg on the ground next to mine and we stood there looking at them.

Then someone yelled, "The train's moving!"

The train inched forward and suddenly the paramedics around Bill flew into action. They hoisted him onto a stretcher and whisked him into the waiting ambulance. His whole body was packed in ice. Sirens blared and the ambulance sped off.

One of the paramedics began looking around where Bill had been lying. "Where's his legs? Where's his legs?" he yelled.

"Over here," said the cop.

The paramedic held out a clear plastic bag. It was a garbage bag.

"You're going to put them in that?" I asked.

"Give me a hand," said the paramedic. "They'll be waiting for these at the hospital."

We stuffed Bill's legs in the bag and they were strapped down in the back of another ambulance, just like they were another person.

It turned out not to matter what we did with those stray legs because the doctors at the hospital determined that it wouldn't be possible to reattach them to Bill's body. The doctors said that Bill was a lucky man, though, because the train's wheels had sliced him quite cleanly, and if the wheel hadn't stopped right on top of him, he would have bled to death out on those tracks.

Bill spent four months in the hospital and on the day he got out, he was arrested. Phylis said she planned to press charges regardless of what kind of shape he was in. Bill got a two-year sentence for felony assault, plus the Missouri-Pacific line slapped him with a charge for disrupting progress on the tracks.

One day I received a postcard from Bill. It said: "Things are going well here in the penitentiary. I got a tattoo and I'm getting my head straight. Please visit. Love, Bill."

I decided to go and see him. I had only visited him once in the hospital and he was in pretty bad shape then. He kept throwing up into a bucket and calling me a wussy.

When I got to the prison I went up to one of the wardens and said, "I'm here to see Bill McQuill."

The warden sort of chuckled. "Oh, that guy."

I was led into the visitors' center where I sat down in one of the chairs lined up in a long row. There was a set of booths with a wall of glass between me and the actual prison. Bill strolled in on the other side with a broad smile on his face. I was surprised to see how well he got around. Those long arms were a real advantage to him now. He walked upright on his hands just like they were two feet, his waistline hovering just inches above the cement floor. He padded along like that and hoisted himself up into a chair. We sat there facing each other with the glass wall between us. Bill looked just like a regular person, except that he was cut off at the waist. He'd lost some weight as well.

"It's good to see you Bill," I said. "You look great."

"Well," said Bill, "I'm half the man I used to be."

"That's pretty funny."

"I know it is."

"How come you don't use a wheelchair, or some of those plastic legs?"

"Prosthetics? You think I should use prosthetics?"

"I don't know. Is that what they call them?"

"I get around better on my hands," said Bill. "I'm closer to the ground. Less distance to fall."

"That makes sense."

"I know it does. You want to see my tattoo?"

"Sure."

Bill rolled up his sleeve. The tattoo was on his upper arm. It was drawn in dark blue ink and the lines were kind of fuzzy.

"What is that?" I asked. "A rabbit?"

"It's a train."

"Oh, right. Yeah."

It looked like a child's drawing. Underneath it were the words "Bill McQuill."

"That's nice," I said.

"Thanks," said Bill. "I did it myself."

The pane of glass between us was thick enough to stop bullets. We had to talk through a little wire mesh hole.

"Lean closer," said Bill.

I leaned in closer.

"I want to whisper something in your ear."

"Okay."

I stuck my ear up to the hole.

"Do you think you could bring me some marijuana?" Bill whispered.

"What?"

"Some pot. Bake it into a cake or something."

"I don't know, Bill."

"Next week is my birthday."

There was a guard standing behind Bill. He had firm, military features and he was staring right at us. I glanced up at him and he shook his head at me.

I said to Bill, "I'll see what I can do."

"You'll bake it into a cake?"

"I'll try, Bill," I said.

"And you'll come back next week?"

"Sure, okay. I'll come back."

Bill smiled at me. He glanced around at the hard concrete surroundings and nodded his head up and down, pleased now with the thoughts flowing through his brain.

"Right on," he said to me. "Cool. Wonderful. Knock yourself out . . ."

The Snow Frog

PART I
THE EGG

Elizabeth was in the kitchen with the rest of us, trying once again to do that trick with the egg. I'd been watching her out of the corner of my eye while someone else was talking. She picked up a fairly small egg, a white one from the farm, and she was sort of caressing it with her fingers. She probably knew somebody was watching her. Before she did it she said quietly, "Okay, here goes . . ."

Then she popped the egg, shell and all, into her mouth. She tilted her head back and made a loud gulping sound. I stood up from my chair. So did Tom. He was the oldest person there. He was probably 75 years old. He'd been watching her, too, I guess.

"Don't do that," he said.

But it was too late. Elizabeth's neck was bulging out now, swollen with the presence of that egg. She hadn't even chewed. It just went straight down and lodged itself in her throat. Her eyes popped out wide and I thought about lunging forward and socking her in the stomach so that the egg might shoot back up. But then she gulped again and swallowed it right down into her belly.

"Oh great," said Grace. She was the one who owned the farm. "What are we going to do now?"

"This happened before," said Tom. "She's done this trick before."

"She was okay before," I said.

"Are you okay, Elizabeth?" asked Grace. "Can you breathe now?"

"Yes," said Elizabeth. "I can."

And then she smiled. Elizabeth had thin lips, with hardly any color in them. She was very skinny. Perhaps the egg would break apart in her stomach, I thought. It would nourish her and do her good. I took comfort in this notion as I sipped at my hot chocolate.

Grace's farm was a place for people who couldn't fit in anywhere else. She let us all stay there as long as we did work and stayed out of trouble. A few people, like Tom, had been there for a long time, ten or twenty years. I'd been there for about a year. Elizabeth was the most recent arrival.

A few days after that egg incident Elizabeth and I were out behind the house, standing by the woodpile. Grace had sent us there to clean things up and get the stacks in order for the coming winter. We were just standing there, though, not doing any work.

I put my hand on Elizabeth's bony fingers and leaned a little closer to her. I thought I might try to kiss her. But then she put her hand over her mouth and coughed a little.

"I don't feel so well," she said.

"Oh, okay," I said.

"I think I need to sit down."

"All right."

But before she could sit down she coughed again. She held on to her belly and I thought she was going to throw up. Her throat made this raspy noise and now it seemed like she might be choking on something.

"Are you choking?" I asked her.

Elizabeth doubled over and retched. Her thin body heaved and a small object popped out of her mouth and into her hands. Her hair was covering her face and I couldn't see what it was.

Then she stood up and held her hands out to me. There, cupped within them, was a little baby chick. It was wet from her saliva, but it was moving, alive.

"You gave birth, Elizabeth," I said.

"I know," she said. "Look at that."

The tiny chick squeaked and flapped its wings a little.

"Let's take it to the chicken coop," said Elizabeth. "One of them will take care of it. That's a good idea, don't you think?"

"Sure," I said. "I think so."

We walked over to the chicken coop with Elizabeth cradling the chick carefully in her two hands.

"Don't tell anyone about this," she said to me. "I want for this to be a secret."

"Okay Elizabeth," I said, "I won't tell anybody at all . . ."

PART II
WHAT TOM FOUND

Tom and I were down in the barn finishing up the chores from the list Grace had given us. Tom was talking to the animals, as he always did, saying things like, "How now brown cow?" or "What's shakin' bacon?" He'd say that to the pigs. He was a fairly funny guy for an old man.

I was raking hay from one of the stalls and Tom went out to the pig's trough to empty it and hose it down. I heard him say, "Hey, are those worms or snakes?"

"What?" I said.

"Come here."

I went outside and saw him bent over the trough, staring down at something in the muck. I joined him there, looking down. That's when I saw what he was talking about. There were little bodies in there, long and rounded, like puffy sausages. They were pale and translucent, slightly green. About a dozen of them were wobbling about in a small pile among the food scraps and sour milk. A clear, jelly-like goo surrounded them, holding their bodies together.

"I don't think those are snakes," I said.

"Neither do I," said Tom.

"Maybe they're larvae," I said.

"You don't even know what larvae is," said Tom.

"Well, they don't look like worms."

"Big worms maybe."

"Do you think the pigs ate them?" I asked.

"I hope not," said Tom.

We decided not to tell Grace about these creatures. "She worries too much," said Tom. "She'll make us spray the whole place down with poison."

Tom took his shovel and scooped the big worms into a plastic bucket and we carried them across the fields and out into the woods where we dumped them into a ditch. I was going to cover them up with dirt but Tom said not to do that.

"Don't bury things alive," he said to me. "It's not right."

Elizabeth and I were in the barn after dinner. It was dark out and we had lit a candle. Once again, I wanted to try to kiss her, but she didn't seem interested. She was sitting on a bale of hay, bouncing up and down and looking around the barn.

"Hey," I said, "would you like to see what Tom and I found this afternoon?"

"Yes, I would," said Elizabeth.

I knew that Tom wouldn't be happy with me for

telling Elizabeth, but I was at a loss for interesting things to say. I wanted to show her something impressive. I picked up the candle and told Elizabeth to follow me. Together we walked out toward the spot in the woods where Tom and I had left the worms. I carried the candle with me and I tried to hold my hand up in front of the flame so that the wind wouldn't blow it out. This was difficult to do because I was excited and walking quickly. Eventually the wind sneaked around my fingers and the flame went out.

In the darkness up ahead I spotted the ditch we had dug. It was easy to see because there was a dim green light coming from inside it. It looked like someone had lit a small campfire at the bottom of the hole.

"This is it," I said to Elizabeth.

We walked over to the hole and gazed down at the worms. They were quivering together in a little mass, still covered in that jelly. Their inner organs glowed green through their pale skin. That's where the green light came from, their insides.

"Oh wow," said Elizabeth. She got down on her knees and scooped one up. She had to use two hands because it was so slippery. Tom and I hadn't touched them that afternoon. We had been too afraid.

"Careful," I said. "Did it sting you?"

"No," said Elizabeth. "It feels warm."

She held it up and her skinny face was illuminated by the worm's green light. Her teeth appeared green when she smiled. Elizabeth handed the worm to me. It seemed bigger now, about the size of a hot dog. It felt soft and warm, like it was filled with heated pudding.

"What is it?" I asked her.

"A glow worm," said Elizabeth, "a giant one."

The worm slipped out of my hands and fell onto the ground. A little bit of glowing liquid dropped onto my boot.

"I hope they aren't poisonous," I said.

"Me, too," said Elizabeth.

With the tip of her shoe she pushed the stray worm back into the hole with the others. "It needs the others to stay warm," she said.

We watched the worms crawl upon each other and twist their glowing bodies around in a jellied pile. A cold wind picked up and Elizabeth moved closer to me.

"We'd better head back," she said.

She was right. Grace would be expecting us at the house. The temperature was dropping. I could feel it. It was nearly winter. I took Elizabeth's hand and we walked back through the woods and across the fields together.

PART III

WINTER COMES

"It's snowing."

Early in the morning Elizabeth stood next to my bed shaking my arm with her cold fingers.

"Look outside," she said.

I sat up and saw that the ground was covered in deep white. It was the first snow of the year. The ground had been bare when we went to bed and I wondered how so much snow had fallen in just one night.

Grace was downstairs preparing a warm breakfast. Some of the others were already awake. Elizabeth looked at me with wide eyes.

"The worms," she said. "They'll freeze."

"We'll check them after breakfast," I said.

It was my job to start the wood furnace. I went down to the basement and got it going. By the time I was done, everyone upstairs had eaten most of the eggs. I looked around the kitchen for Elizabeth.

"She's not here," said Grace.

Tom looked up at me and shook his head. I think he knew I'd told Elizabeth about the worms. I grabbed a piece of toast and went outside.

It was still snowing—big blankets of it rushed across the field. I could see Elizabeth's footprints leading toward the woods. The wind had almost smoothed them over and erased her tracks. I pushed forward, following the faded path into the trees. The snowflakes melted on my face and dripped down my shirt.

Elizabeth was kneeling down digging in the snow when I found her. I got down beside her and dug, too. I'd forgotten to wear gloves so my hands got cold quickly.

"Where are they?" she asked me.

"Maybe they crawled away," I said. "Maybe they found someplace warm."

"I don't think so," she said.

My hand hit upon something hard, like a small stone. I dug more and uncovered the pile of them, all frozen together, no longer glowing. Now they were a dull, sickly yellow color, like rotten fruit.

Elizabeth began to cry. Then I did, too. I wasn't that sad about them dying, I just didn't like the way it looked, the pile of them there, helpless in the snow. And my hands were numb with the cold.

Elizabeth gathered up the hardened bodies and held them in the front of her sweater, the way you carry apples.

"I'm bringing them home," she said.

Down in the basement, Elizabeth laid the worms out in neat rows next to the wood furnace. She thought they might thaw out in the heat and resurrect themselves. The worms had grown larger before they died. Some of them had developed little pointed tails and rounded heads. It seemed possible that they weren't really worms at all, but there was no point in dwelling on that.

"Don't let Grace see this," I said to her.

"Don't worry," said Elizabeth.

Tom poked his head downstairs and looked over the limp bodies.

"They grew," he said.

"But now they're dead," I pointed out.

"Well," said Tom, "that's what happens."

The worms did not revive as Elizabeth had hoped. They just got wet and droopy and began to smell a little. Tom, Elizabeth, and I went out behind the barn and buried them the next day. We found a patch of mud where the snow had melted and we dug the grave. Elizabeth said a quiet prayer and I shoveled the wet mud over their bodies.

"It's okay to bury them now," said Tom. "Now it's proper."

PART IV
INCUBATOR

I was brushing my teeth in the bathroom and Elizabeth knocked on the wooden door. I let her in and she shut it behind her. She was barefoot and wearing a thin white nightgown, the kind you could almost see straight through. Her eyes were wild and excited.

"What's going on?" I asked her.

Elizabeth said, "Shhhh," and turned out the light.

"Look," she said to me.

Elizabeth stood before me like a ghost, all white in her flimsy gown. Except for her stomach. It was glowing green, just a little. I could make out the faint shape of one of those worms, nestled snugly underneath her skin just below her belly button. The worm was illuminated, alive, and growing inside of her.

"You ate one," I said.

"That's right," she said. "I swallowed it down when it was frozen and hard."

"It's still alive."

"Just like the egg," she said. "It turned into a chick."

Elizabeth took my hand and guided it onto her belly. It was very, very warm.

PART V
CHRISTMAS

Tom's job was to kill a turkey for the Christmas dinner. Elizabeth and I went with him to the pen where the birds were kept and helped him pick one out. We hadn't told anyone about her worm, not even Tom. The winter weather allowed her to wear bulky sweaters which concealed the radiant bulge within her belly.

Together we looked over the flock of birds and chose a big one—not the biggest, but a good sized one—for our dinner.

Before he took it down to the slaughterhouse Tom said to both of us, "You know, if there's anything you don't want to discuss with Grace, you can always bring it up with me first."

He gave a quick nod toward Elizabeth's belly and then went off to wrestle the bird into its cage. I guess that worm wasn't so well hidden after all.

The next night, after the big turkey dinner, Elizabeth and I were supposed to do the dishes, but she could barely stand up. She held on to the edge of the sink and wiped the sweat from her forehead with a rag.

"I'm not feeling well," she said.

Grace felt her forehead and pulled her hand away quickly. "You're hot," she said. "You'd better go lie down."

"Okay," said Elizabeth. She stumbled up the stairs and into her bed.

"She probably ate too much," I said.

Grace pursed her lips and nodded. Then she set to work on the dishes with me.

Tom woke me up near midnight. He was standing over my bed, fully dressed.

"Wake up," he said.

We went down to the kitchen where Elizabeth was rolled up into a ball on the floor, clutching her stomach.

"I'm hot," she moaned. "I'm burning up."

I was afraid she'd wake everybody in the house. I picked up her heated body and carried her outside. Tom followed me. It was a clear winter night. The snow was deep and the stars gave everything a pale hue.

"Let's go to the barn," said Tom.

We laid her down upon some hay and Tom placed a cool, wet towel on her forehead. The animals shifted about in their stalls, neighing and grunting at our presence.

Elizabeth rolled over onto her back and it was then that her bathrobe dropped open and Tom saw the glowing shape within her belly. He stared at it quietly for a moment. Then he looked at me.

"She ate one," I said.

"So I see," he said.

The bulge was pretty large now, about the size of a melon, and it was glowing brightly. We could feel the heat coming from it as we knelt down next to her.

The animals began to make a lot of noise, kicking the ground and pushing each other in their pens. Tom went over to calm them. "Oh hey," he said to them. He let a few of the sheep out so that they would quit banging on the walls. Some pigs wandered around as well.

Elizabeth started to cough and grabbed her stomach. She rolled onto her hands and knees and began that same retching sound I'd heard before, when we were out behind the woodpile.

"It's coming up," I said to Tom. I patted Elizabeth softly on the back. I said to her, "You'll be okay," although I wasn't really so sure.

Her retching grew louder and then it stopped. Her muscles tightened and a few short squeaks escaped from her mouth.

"She's choking," said Tom.

"Can you breathe?" I asked Elizabeth.

She pounded her hands on the ground and put her head down like she was saying some kind of prayer. The pigs squealed and ran away from her. Her whole body convulsed in strange spasms. Still, nothing came out of her.

"She's going to pass out," I said.

Tom stepped forward and placed his arms around her waist. He lifted her up and locked his hands together under her stomach. Elizabeth's face turned blue and her eyes rolled back in her head.

"Help her, Tom," I said.

Tom jerked his arms together. It was the Heimlich maneuver, just like we'd all been taught. Some green goo spurted out from Elizabeth's mouth.

"Do it again," I said.

Tom yanked again and more goo flew out of her mouth. Then she coughed and a deep monstrous belch rose up within her. Tom let her go and suddenly she was on her hands and knees again. Her body heaved and out of her mouth poured forth buckets of the green goo, more than I would ever have thought could be inside her. Then, slowly, the glowing shape emerged. Its bulbous tip poked forth from Elizabeth's mouth and her jaw seemed almost to unhinge in order to allow its passage. The green blob plopped out onto the barn floor and began to squirm. Elizabeth gasped, sucking in an enormous breath of air. Then she fell onto her side.

The glowing form which had spouted from Elizabeth's mouth wriggled about before us. It was covered in a filmy membrane sack, its limbs poking away at it from the inside, struggling to break free.

"Help it," said Elizabeth. "Do something."

I crept forward on my knees and touched my finger lightly upon the slimy skin. The whole blob was about the size of a large grapefruit. Whatever was inside really wanted to get out. I stuck two fingers into the membrane and hooked them around it. Then I pulled back, tearing a little hole in the surface.

A long, thin leg emerged, and then another. Elizabeth sat up and moved closer to me. Tom stood quietly behind us. The membrane sack slipped away and there before us, among the goo and slime on the barn's floor, stood a very large, glowing frog.

It stared at us with two enormous glassy eyes, its long legs tucked neatly under its slimy body. It was glowing very brightly now, giving off a green hue so strong that it lit up the entire barn. It was warm, too, as if we were sitting in front of a small fire.

"That's the most beautiful frog I've ever seen," said Elizabeth.

"He's very handsome," said Tom.

The frog turned and hopped away from us, heading toward the door.

"Open it up," said Elizabeth. "He wants to go outside."

I stood up and opened the big barn door for him. The cool air rushed in and a little snow blew into the barn. I was worried that this would bother the frog, but he didn't mind at all. He paused at the snow-covered field before him, and then he hopped forward, taking big leaps into the air and landing softly on his strong legs. When he stood still, the snow around him began to melt, such was the heat he gave off from his skin.

Tom, Elizabeth, and I went out to the field to join him and we spent much of the night following him around and marveling at the amazing sight of his glowing body hopping through the fields of snow. We decided then that he would be called The Snow Frog.

Over the next few days the frog grew larger, fed steadily on a diet of slop and beans which he shared with the pigs in their trough. He preferred to sleep after his morning meal, and he wouldn't wake until nightfall, when he liked to venture out into the fields and hop about, glowing green under the winter moon. When he reached the size of the smaller piglets, about twenty to thirty pounds, he stopped growing.

Of course, now you see snow frogs which are much bigger than this original member of the species. Some of them are as large as full-size hounds. And the sight of them bounding through the snow, glowing brightly on cold winter nights, is almost commonplace in the North Country and high alpine regions. The children in these rural towns and villages are often heard begging their parents' permission to stay up late so that they may run out to the fields and play happily with the good-natured beasts. There is no vision more wonderful to me than the sight of these children around Christmastime frolicking in the snow with those warm, fat, glowing frogs.

Little Rodney

Oh, how I did admire that Carla Brown. She was a woman who lived next door to me, on a quiet, tree-lined street in central Texas. She was an auto body mechanic and she did most of her work right out there in her front yard, pounding away at metal slabs and slicing them up with a blowtorch in the noonday sun. Carla lived alone with a small, three-legged dog named Rodney. Rodney was not very fond of me.

I had, on a few occasions, tried to ask Carla out on dates. It would go something like this:

"Hi, Carla. That's nice work you're doing on that car."

And she would say, "Thanks a lot."

Then I'd say, "Hey, how would you like to get something to eat with me?"

"Yeah, well, see," she'd say, "I've kind of given up eating solid foods. I'm trying to get away from all that these days."

"Okay, yeah, sure," I'd say. "I understand completely."

Of course, I didn't understand completely. I had no idea what she was talking about. But even so, I couldn't help admiring her.

Often Carla hung around with a large bearded man known as Jed. She told me he was just a friend. Jed liked to call me "Willy" even though that is not my name.

One day Jed drove over in his blue van and parked it in front of Carla's place. Carla walked out with a large backpack over her shoulder and threw it inside the van. Little three-legged Rodney followed after her. I heard Jed and Carla arguing about something and then there was a knock on my door. I opened it and there stood Carla and Rodney. The little dog eyed me suspiciously.

"I need to ask you a favor," said Carla.

"Okay," I said.

"It's only for a little while, a short trip," she said. "We'll be back soon."

"Okay," I said again.

So Carla pushed Rodney inside my house and ran off to join Jed and his van. I watched them drive away and then turned to look at Rodney, who sat dumbfounded on my kitchen floor.

"Grrrrrr," he said.

I made up my mind that Rodney and I would become pals. The truth was, I could have used a little companionship. Although I did happen to know that Rodney wasn't fond of me now, I figured this situation could change. And if it did, then so too might Carla's seemingly neutral feelings toward me.

Not far from my house was an area of public land known to all of us as Cuervo Gardens. The "garden" part of the name was misleading. It was a square mile of thickets and brambles and dry rock creek beds where folks liked to drive around and drink hard liquor. I took Rodney out there and let him hop about after the toads and lizards and rabbits which inhabited the land. Although I felt that Rodney's hyperactive demeanor left something to be desired, I had to admire his resourcefulness for a dog with only three legs. He was so agile, you would have thought he preferred those three legs to four.

At some point that afternoon Rodney scampered off after an armadillo and I didn't see him again for the rest of the day. In fact, I didn't see him again for quite some time. I called out his name for hours, but night fell and still he did not return.

"Shit," I thought.

I went home and drew a picture of Rodney on a piece of paper, taking pains to accurately portray his three-legged nature. Underneath the crude figure I wrote the words: "Missing, one three-legged dog—REWARD if found." I made copies of this flyer and tacked them up all over the neighborhood.

The next day I got a call from an elderly woman. She told me that she had Rodney in her custody.

"I understand you are offering a reward," she said.

"Yes, I am," I said.

About an hour later a gray station wagon pulled up to my house. The woman at the wheel was very small. Her head barely reached over the dashboard. She wore enormous black sunglasses. Sitting behind her in the back of the wagon was a metal cage covered by a towel.

"Let's see the money," said the woman.

"No," I said. "Let's see the dog."

The woman sighed and stepped out of her vehicle. She really was a tiny lady, only about half my size. She opened up the back door and undid the latch to the cage. A little brown mutt dashed out and began running around in circles on the street.

"That dog has four legs," I said.

"I know that," said the woman.

"The dog I'm looking for has three legs," I said. "I wrote that specifically on the flyer."

The old woman removed her giant sunglasses and peered down at the dog.

"Well, then," she said, "I suppose your dog must have sprouted another leg."

I told her this was not the case and I refused to give her the reward, as we had previously agreed. She tried to bargain with me, lowering her asking price significantly, but I held firm.

The morning passed by and Rodney remained missing. Each time I heard a car rumble down our street I feared it would be Carla and Jed returning early from their trip. I would have to explain to them my failure. I pictured big Jed shaking his bearded head and saying, "Aw, Willy, you really fucked it up this time."

So I drove back over to Cuervo Gardens and parked my car in the shade so as to avoid the glaring heat of the afternoon sun. I sat on the hood and called out Rodney's name over and over. I strained my ears listening for the jingle of his collar, or maybe a muted bark, but there was nothing. I was about to pack it in and leave when I heard a woman's voice off in the distance.

"Isabella! Isabella!" she called out. Then she began to whistle, like she too was calling for a dog.

Another abandoned soul, I thought, out searching for her pet! She was far away, but getting closer, calling out the name "Isabella!" every few seconds.

I began to wonder if perhaps the land around here contained some kind of vortex into which wayward dogs sometimes slipped and never returned. Poor Isabella, I thought. Poor Rodney!

I wandered away from the car toward the woman's voice. I wanted to talk to her, to commiserate over our regrettable circumstances. But as I made my way through the bushes and brambles I got a little lost myself. Now I couldn't make out where that voice was coming from at all.

I was about to call out to her when I heard a muted bark. A short little "Yip!" Then there was a sort of "Arp!" Was it Rodney? I couldn't tell. Perhaps it was Isabella. I wouldn't mind finding her, either, I thought.

I ran toward the sound I had heard. I pushed my way through low-lying branches and marched over gravel beds filled with dead cacti.

And then, up ahead, I saw my car. It was parked in the shade where I had left it. I walked closer and saw that there was something large lying on the ground in front of my vehicle. It hadn't been there when I'd left. At first, I thought it was a pile of trash, a long row of flattened plastic garbage bags someone had thoughtlessly dumped while I was away.

But, no, this was not the case at all.

There, stretched out in the shade by my car, lay an enormous snake. A giant snake. Not just a snake, but a python, a giant python of extremely large proportions. It was longer than my car. Its head was as big as a watermelon, its body thicker than my thigh. Its skin was shiny and scaled, covered in elaborate, pulsating patterns.

"Motherfucker," I said.

For now I saw something else which shook me to my very soul. There was a lump in that snake, right in the middle of its body—a motionless lump just about the size of a dog.

I studied it from a distance, trying to judge whether the animal inside that snake was Rodney. Did it have three legs? The lump appeared to move, as if whatever was beneath that scaly skin was struggling to get out. Little Rodney! My tenacious pal, swallowed alive like Jonah himself!

The big snake's eyes were glassy and calm. I have heard that after a snake devours its prey, it lies in a near comatose state, its energy thoroughly expended in the effort it takes to digest a creature alive. This was my chance.

I crept closer to the beast, noting the sly position of its mouth. Why do all snakes seem to smile? This is what I was thinking when the snake lifted its head and then shot forward at me. Perhaps that digestion theory had been wrong.

There was no time to deliberate now, no time to weigh the prudencey of my actions. The battle was upon me. I dodged the lunging head of the python and slipped around to its back side. I grabbed hold of its massive tail and heaved with all my might. The power of that beast! Right there in my very hands!

"DOGEATER!" I cried, "RODNEY, I SHALL AVENGE YOU!"

It was a mighty struggle, but I did prevail, smashing the snake's body repeatedly onto the hard rocky earth. In the end, its great body lay limp on the ground before me.

At first, when I heard the cries of the woman, I assumed it was the snake, calling out for mercy, begging for me to stop. But then, of course, I realized that snakes cannot talk, or even make any sounds for that matter.

Standing behind me, just a few feet away, was a

dark-haired, pale-skinned young woman, her face full of shock and anger.

"You've killed Isabella," she said to me.

Now, here I must admit to having earlier fallen prey to the temptation of slight exaggeration. That snake was not quite as long nor perhaps quite as thick as I had first described. As I stood there above its limp body I realized that indeed it was a household pet, a snake accustomed to shag carpets and manmade tree limbs. Isabella here probably could not have fit Rodney into her mouth after all.

"I've made a mistake," I said.

I touched Isabella with the tip of my foot, hoping that she would slither back to life, but she did not.

"I thought she ate a dog," I explained. "My friend's dog is missing and I saw a lump in her belly."

"Isabella is pregnant," said the woman. "Her belly is full of babies."

Together we loaded the snake into my car. I drove as fast as I could to the animal hospital where skilled and caring surgeons removed Isabella's soft, damaged eggs one by one.

"She was looking for a place to lay her eggs," the woman explained to me. "That was why she left home. That's why I was looking for her."

"I'm very sorry for what I have done," I said. I said it over and over to her.

We sat together in the waiting room, me and this snake-loving woman. "Perhaps the eggs will survive," I told her. "We can raise them together. They'll be bigger and more beautiful than even Isabella."

"Perhaps," said the woman.

I took hold of her hand and she let it sit there, inside of mine, soft and motionless.

"Maybe if we say a prayer," I said. "That might help."

"Okay," said the woman.

I was unaccustomed to prayer, and I suspected the woman was as well, but we bowed our heads all the same, and together we said a little prayer for the unborn snakes.

It was about a week after that when I finally heard the tiny scratching on my front door. I opened it up and there stood Rodney, skinny and shivering on his three little legs. I stepped aside and he hopped forward into my house, wagging his bony tail, glad to see me. I cooked up some ground beef which had been sitting in my refrigerator and I mixed it in a bowl with potatoes and brown gravy. Little Rodney ate until he could eat no more. Then he passed out on the kitchen floor, fat-bellied and content.

Carla Brown and her boyfriend Jed never did return.

Beach Trip

I saw Elizabeth driving her rusty red station wagon down Union Street in the middle of the day. Her large black dog, Willis, was panting away in the backseat. It was summer, one of those hot days where the tar on the road gets soft and smells funny. She didn't have air-conditioning in her car and I was afraid that Willis might die.

Elizabeth stopped the car beside me and I asked her, "Is he going to be okay?"

"He's fine," said Elizabeth. "Get inside. We're going to the beach."

I hadn't been planning on going to the beach, or even spending the day with Elizabeth for that matter, but like I said, it was hot. So I got in the car.

As it turned out, I had been right to worry about Willis. Shortly into our drive he lay down on his side and barfed all over the backseat.

"Oh shit," said Elizabeth.

We pulled over and tried to revive him. Willis was a big Newfoundland, the kind of dog they used on missions to the North Pole. We lifted him out of the car and I poured water on his head while Elizabeth fanned his face with a newspaper. While we were doing this a small sports car pulled over next to us and a little man wearing sunglasses got out.

"What seems to be the problem?" he asked us.

"My dog overheated," said Elizabeth.

"I see," said the man.

Poor Willis was just lying there in the dirt by the road. The man leaned over and placed his hand on Willis's neck. He pushed his fingers around as if he were feeling for a pulse, or maybe he was checking his glands.

"I'm a licensed veterinarian," said the man.

"Oh," said Elizabeth.

The man finished his examination and returned to his vehicle to fetch a leather duffel bag, the kind old-time doctors used when they made house calls.

"Today is your lucky day," he said to us. He reached inside the bag and produced an orange plastic vial which was filled with little pills. He emptied four of these pills into his hand.

"I'm going to give him two of these right now," said the veterinarian. "I'd like you to administer the other two in a few hours."

"What is it?" I asked him.

The veterinarian placed the two tablets on Willis's

outstretched tongue and then held the dog's mouth shut so that he was forced to swallow.

"They're for the heat," replied the vet. And with that he handed Elizabeth the other two tablets, hopped back into his sports car, and drove away.

Willis coughed a little, but then he sat up and seemed to be revived almost immediately. We cleaned the barf off the seat and loaded him back into the car.

"Well," said Elizabeth, "let's get to the beach."

Elizabeth drove on and I examined the little pills the vet had given her. They were light blue, an electric shade which seemed to glow, even in the daylight.

"What do you think is inside them?" I asked her.

"You heard the man," said Elizabeth, "they're for the heat."

"Oh, right," I said.

The beach was long and beautiful. I'd forgotten how nice a beach can be. There were waves curling up and crashing down right onto the sandy shore. Little children scurried about with plastic toys and inflatable flotation devices. We got out of the car into the bright sun and big Willis ran straight away for the water. Elizabeth and I walked in the sand. We had to bury our feet with each step because the surface was so hot. The beach was not too crowded and everyone there knew how lucky they were. Probably the whole interior of the country was burning up right then in the heat, but those of us here by the seaside, we were going to be okay.

We sat down on a blanket and ate some sandwiches which Elizabeth had made. Then we went swimming with full stomachs, a course of action which I knew from my childhood was not proper, but we did all right. Willis swam around with us. He was so pleased at this turn of events—from a hot car to the beach! Yes!

Elizabeth and I got out of the water and lay down on the blanket. We fell asleep and when we woke up almost everyone who'd been at the beach was gone. Willis was wandering around eating the food scraps and garbage they'd left behind.

"Well, look at this," said Elizabeth.

"How long were we asleep?" I asked.

"I don't know," said Elizabeth.

The sun had started to set. It was no longer hot out.

"We forgot to give Willis his pills," I said.

"He doesn't need them anymore," said Elizabeth.

She was right. Willis was fine now. Elizabeth reached into her bag and found the two electric blue pills. She held them in her palm where they glowed brightly in the dim light. With two fingers, Elizabeth picked up one of the pills and dropped it into her mouth. She swallowed it without any water. Then she held the other one out for me.

"Okay," I said, and I swallowed mine down, too.

We watched the sun finish setting, which seemed to take a very long time. Then it was dark and we could hear the waves rumbling just a few feet away.

"The tide is coming in," I said. "We're going to get wet."

"No, we're not," said Elizabeth. "The water is miles away."

Minutes later a wave came along and we got soaked.

"Shit," said Elizabeth. "Fuck."

Willis ambled over to us, whining to go home.

"I can't drive now," said Elizabeth, "can you?"

"No," I said, "I'm afraid I can't." That blue pill had made me feel queasy and strange.

"We'll have to sleep here tonight," said Elizabeth.

"That would be nice," I said.

We moved our wet belongings up away from the surf and lay down upon them. Elizabeth began to touch me on the face and on my chest. We were just friends so this was unusual. Then we started kissing. She had a nice strong tongue, or that's the way it seemed to me.

"Pretend I'm a mermaid and you found me here on the beach," said Elizabeth.

I tried to do that, picturing her with a sexy fish's bottom and an innocent mythical face. I rubbed up against her and felt her nice breasts. Her skin tasted like salt. It was all goose bumped from the cold, or maybe she was excited. I was excited, too, but then I thought, Who makes love to a mermaid right after he's found her? What kind of jerk would do that? We both got tired and fell asleep covered in sand and bits of kelp.

I woke up at dawn, alone on the beach. Elizabeth

and Willis were gone, and so was her car. They'd left me here, miles from where I lived. I sat up and looked out at the ocean, calm and serene now at this early hour. I decided to go for a swim, all by myself, and walked out into the water. I liked the taste of salt water and I liked how cold the ocean was against my skin. I believe we are all very lucky these days that the sea is still here for us, that we can still immerse ourselves inside its amazing belly during the unbearable heat of the day.

Chainsaw Apple

It seemed like a pretty simple trick to me. My friend Robert would hold the apple in his mouth while I, steady-handed, carved his initials into the piece of fruit with a chainsaw. "It only looks dangerous," I told Robert. "You have nothing at all to worry about."

Of course, I practiced first. I speared an apple on the end of a stick and took the chainsaw to it then. The stick was not an adequate brace, however, and the apple went spinning off across the yard as soon as I touched it with the saw. Such an excellent instrument, the chainsaw—power, speed, and grace, all in one package. I've seen those folks who use chainsaws to carve majestic swans out of a block of ice. I tried to do that, too, but I had no patience for it in the end. A swan's neck is so delicate.

Vicegrips turned out to be a good substitute for the human mouth. Robert looked on from a distance as I began to perfect my technique. A light tap with just the tip of the blade was all that I needed to make a mark. The saw cut so easily through the apple's flesh. But the little curve in the letter R was a problem for me. To make matters worse, Robert's last name was Ulfburg and the challenge there was to carve that U without making it look like a V.

"I wish your name was Xavier Lewis," I told him.

I believe that most practitioners of chainsaw tricks use small utility chainsaws, the kind deigned for saplings and shearing thin limbs off trees. I, myself, own a Lumberman 650, which happens to be a very large and unwieldy instrument. I bought it some years ago with the intention of using it to level the great oaks and pine trees in my backyard. I would have firewood for years to come, I thought. Only one tree fell victim to the great saw, however. It seems those big oaks and pines actually belonged to my neighbor.

Robert suggested I trade in my large saw for a set of three smaller ones. Then I could learn to juggle them as well. It wasn't a bad idea, but first things first, I needed to master this trick. Besides, I had a feeling the effect might be lost if I used something small and wimpy. The Lumberman 650's bite on the apple was really pretty spectacular. It splattered little shards of fruit everywhere.

After a few days of practice I felt that I was ready. I called up Robert and told him to bring over some safety goggles. I didn't want him to get apple stuck in his eye. Upon his arrival, Robert expressed reservations once again about the size of the Lumberman 650. Don't be ridiculous, I told him. But when Robert stuck the apple in his mouth I could see that he had a point. Robert is a tall man, well over six feet, and I had a little trouble lifting the heavy saw up to the height of his mouth. When I finally did get it up high enough, I lost all my leverage and the motion of the chain caused the tool to jiggle and sway. I touched the tip of the blade to the apple, sending little chunks of fruit flying right up Robert's nose. He recoiled, spitting out the apple and sneezing uncontrollably.

"Maybe some noseplugs," I suggested.

In addition to the plugs, I decided Robert should kneel down on his knees. This way I wouldn't have such a hard time getting the saw up to the right height. This also had the added benefit of making it appear as if Robert was about to be beheaded, like in a medieval execution.

I was much better at holding the chainsaw still now that Robert's mouth was down at a more manageable level. I sliced into the apple with my first vertical stroke and Robert shut his eyes tight. Clear, fizzing apple juice dribbled down his chin. I continued my work, easing into the delicate curves. Robert did a fine job of holding still, but even so, his head had a little more give than those vicegrips I'd been practicing with. In the end, my RU looked more like an F and a Y.

"We'll have to practice some more before we go public with this trick," I explained to Robert.

Three days later, after several more practice sessions, I saw our opportunity. Over at Speedy's Grill they were having a Memorial Day barbecue and there were sure to be many people there. Speedy's has a little outdoor stage by the picnic tables and folks would often hop up there and sing songs or make announcements. I figured this would be a fine spot to make our debut.

In order to add flavor and spontaneity to the act, I told Robert to arrive at Speedy's at a different time from me. I pretended I had come there alone and didn't know him at all. When I sensed that the crowd was at its peak, I grabbed my duffel bag and jumped up onstage. I yanked the Lumberman 650 out of the bag and revved it up. This, of course, got everyone's attention pretty quick.

"Ladies and gentlemen," I called out, "I'd like to show you all a trick!"

They weren't sure what to make of me, I could tell. A few of the younger patrons looked pretty frightened, as if they thought maybe I would leap out and lay waste to them all right then and there. It is good to have your audience scared from the start.

"I'm going to need a volunteer," I said. "Anybody out there want to help me with this trick?"

I'd instructed Robert to hold off a bit before he raised his hand. This would help perpetuate the illusion that Robert's participation was merely by chance.

I pulled the apple out of my bag. "What I need someone to do," I explained, "is come up here and hold this apple in his mouth. It's very simple. You hold the apple in your mouth and I'll carve your initials in it with this chainsaw."

I heard a few of them gasp. I revved up the saw again for effect. A couple of people screamed.

"Any volunteers?" I called out again.

It was at this point that Robert was supposed to step up, but instead something unusual happened. This smiling young woman raised her hand and ran up onstage yelling, "Me! Me! Me!"

I looked over at Robert. He was standing in the back, his hand raised meekly in the air. "I believe we have a volunteer in the back," I said.

"No," said the young woman, "I'm right here!"

The crowd around me said, "Yeah, she's right there."

The woman was short, dressed in blue jeans and a snappy cowboy shirt. She had nice, trusting eyes.

What a thing to happen on my debut performance! What could I do? "Okay," I said, "we have a volunteer."

The woman picked up the apple and began to polish it by rubbing it against the leg of her blue jeans. "This is going to be great," she said.

"Sure," I said. I didn't know if I should have her get on her knees on not. It seemed to me she was about the right height as it was.

"Okay," I told her, "go ahead and stick that apple in your mouth."

The woman grinned at me. "You forgot something," she said.

"What's that?"

"My name."

"Oh, yeah," I said. "Tell us your name."

"Betsy Smith," said the woman. She said it nice and loud so that everyone could hear. At this point a pretty large crowd had gathered around. Robert was still standing sheepishly in the back. I wondered if he had anything to do with this last-minute substitution, but when I looked at him he just shrugged his shoulders like he didn't know what was going on.

Betsy stuck the apple in her mouth. She really was excited about this. Some people just like to volunteer, I guess. It felt nice to know that she trusted me. I looked out over the audience to see if anyone was with her, a boyfriend or husband perhaps.

The crowd was riveted. They couldn't take their eyes off me. I gunned the engine on the chainsaw once more and stepped up close to Betsy. I held up the saw and tried to picture my line of attack. Sweet as this Betsy Smith was, the change in plans was definitely inconvenient. I'd practiced for hours and hours on the letters RU, now here I was faced with a B and an S.

I drew a couple of tentative lines in the air, not actually touching the apple, just to get the feel of these new letters. B and S! I was going to have some stern words with Robert Ulfburg when this was all over.

Betsy held still as I sliced into the apple with the first downward stroke. I even thought I saw her red lips curl into a bit of a smile, as much as was possible under the circumstances. I carved cautiously the little lines on the letter B, barely grazing the taught skin of the apple with the spinning chain. Bits of fruit flew everywhere. The effect was magnificent. I could hear the audience screaming over the whine of the saw.

I completed the B rather sloppily, but it was acceptable. I moved on to the S, and as I made that first downward slice I noticed that Betsy's eyes were open. She really wanted to take all this in. What a woman. Then I felt the chainsaw give a funny little kick. The motor stopped, and Betsy dropped to her knees, covering her face with her hands.

Every so often the chain on a chainsaw needs to be replaced and if this simple act of maintenance is overlooked, the chain will eventually snap. This is what happened on that particular day.

"My God," I said.

I put down the saw. Betsy wouldn't remove her hands from her face. Blood began to trickle out from between her fingers. A disaster!

Like most chainsaws the Lumberman 650 is designed to stop running immediately when the chain loses tension. But even so, the loose end of the chain whipped around, causing what I imagined was some pretty serious damage to Betsy's face.

"Call an ambulance!" I yelled.

I think some of the people watching thought it was all part of that act. I could see the confused smiles on their faces.

"The chain broke," I said. "It was an accident."

Someone grabbed me from behind. I heard a gruff voice say, "You son of a bitch." I was pulled away from Betsy.

I ran to my car and followed the ambulance to the hospital. When I got there a cop stepped up to me and said he had a few questions. I didn't want to talk to him. I wanted to see how Betsy was doing.

"What is your relationship to the victim?" asked the cop.

"I just met her today," I told him. "It was an accident."

"I think you'd better come with me," said the cop.

Down at the station they took my statement and put me in a cell. "What about Betsy?" I asked them. "Is she going to be okay?"

The officer said, "Don't you think you should have thought of that before you pulled this little stunt?"

Two hours later Robert showed up. He said he would try to post my bail, but he wasn't sure if he had the money. As he spoke I tried to determine if he was upset with me. After all, it could have been him up there with the apple.

"I think it was all that moisture from the fruit," I said to him. "Over time it corroded the steel links on the chain."

Robert said, "I guess we should have thought of that."

"Right," I said. "A lack of foresight."

Robert told me that my Lumberman 650 was back at his house. The cops were looking for it to use as evidence. He wanted to know if he should let them have it.

"Sure," I said. "I don't want that saw anymore."

"Okay," said Robert. And then he left.

That night, as I lay on my hard wooden cot, I tried to imagine what that chain had actually done to Betsy's face. She had such a nice face.

The next morning a cop woke me up, rattling his keys around. He opened the door to my cell and said, "You can go now."

"What?" I asked him.

"Someone posted your bail," he said.

I rubbed my eyes and stood up. "Was it Robert?" I asked him.

"It was that woman," said the cop, "the one you cut up."

I walked out of the cell and retrieved my belongings from the desk clerk. They had taken away my pen and my set of keys, in case I decided to stab somebody with them while I was locked up. I filled out a few forms, promising to conduct myself in a "safe and reasonable manner," and to not leave the state before the trial date.

I walked out into the sunlight and there I saw Ms. Betsy Smith standing on the jailhouse steps, a dark line of stitches running up her face. The red gash ran from the top of her lip to just below her eye. It was surrounded by discolored skin, bruised brown and purple. I looked down at her hands to see if she had any weapons or objects with which to hit me. But she carried nothing.

"The juices from the fruit," I explained to her, "over time they caused rust and wear on the chain."

"You should take better care of your tools," said Betsy.

"I know," I said.

Betsy smiled a half-crooked smile. It looked painful with her face all stitched and swollen like that. I was glad that the chain hadn't taken out her eye.

"Thanks for posting my bail," I said. "I'd like to pay you back for that, as soon as I can get the money together."

"I can't eat solid foods for a while," said Betsy. "Perhaps you could take me out for a milkshake."

"I'd be glad to," I said.

Betsy slipped her arm around mine and we went off in search of some refreshments, soft and cold.

Dogs

No doubt you'll think I'm strange when I tell you I've been making love with my girlfriend's dog. But that is not my most unsettling secret.

Our affair came about one afternoon through a gradual progression of caressing and snuggling. Neither one of us, me or the dog, knew what to think after it happened. We just sat there kind of surprised at the way things had turned out. We really hadn't thought of each other like that. But then, afterward, whenever we found ourselves alone, we'd slip into it again.

Eventually my girlfriend, Maria, began to notice that my sex drive was down. We live together and there was no hiding it. I just didn't have enough in me for both Maria and the dog. I was afraid Maria suspected another woman, but I couldn't tell her the truth.

The dog, by the way, was a little hound-mix, sleek, spotted, and soft. Her name was Ellouise.

It was hard enough to deal with my decreased sex

drive, but then Ellouise began behaving in a way which threatened to blow our cover once and for all. She was getting jealous. Whenever Maria and I got amorous, Ellouise would begin to growl. When Maria and I cuddled on the couch, Ellouise would jump up between us. One night, as we lay sleeping on the bed, I felt a warm tongue licking at my thigh. It was Ellouise, right there in front of Maria! I sat up and pretended to be shocked.

"Ellouise, what are you doing?" I asked.

Luckily, Maria was asleep.

I tried to talk to Ellouise and make her see the difficulty of our situation. I tried to explain that our little affair was nothing more than a fling, but I'm afraid she didn't understand. She barked at me when I protested, and it was all I could do to keep our lovemaking discreet.

One day, while I was at work, I got a call from Maria.

"Have you noticed a change in Ellouise?" she asked me.

"No, not really," I said.

"Are you sure?"

"Yes," I said.

"I took her to the vet today," said Maria.

"You did?"

"Yes," said Maria. "Ellouise is pregnant."

"My God," I said, "I can't believe it."

"Neither can I," said Maria. "I thought we'd kept an eye on her."

"We did."

"She's due in three weeks," said Maria.

"Three weeks?"

"Yes," said Maria. "Who would've guessed?"

"Not me."

I did some research and learned that the gestation period for dogs is about eight weeks long. I thought back over my affair with Ellouise and realized that our first encounter was just about five weeks ago. Had I gotten her pregnant the first time?

I tried calling a few veterinarians. I asked them, anonymously of course, about the possibility of conception between a man and a dog, but they all took it as some kind of prank. I couldn't get a straight answer.

I rushed home and took Ellouise into the bedroom so I could consult with her in private. "Tell me the truth," I said. "Has there been anyone else?"

Maria walked in and said, "Why are you talking to the dog?"

"I was just trying to find out who the father is," I said.

"Well," said Maria, "let me know if she tells you."

Three weeks later Maria and I were sitting in the living room when Ellouise dashed outside and began to dig about under the porch.

"She's making a nest under there," said Maria. "She's getting ready to give birth."

I thought about confessing to Maria right then, just to preempt the shock she would inevitably feel upon seeing my features attached to a litter of puppies, but I didn't have the courage. Also, I still hoped that maybe it was actually some stray canine who had impregnated Ellouise.

That night, as we stood on the porch, we heard the first muted cries of Ellouise's offspring. I listened carefully for any sounds vaguely human, but I couldn't tell.

"I think you should go under there," said Maria. "Bring them inside."

"Okay," I said.

I grabbed a flashlight and crawled under the porch. There wasn't much space. Maria stood above calling out directions through the cracks.

"They're over here," she said.

I shimmied my way across the dirt and shined my light upon the pups. There sat Ellouise with a litter of squirming little bodies. I crept closer. They all appeared quite doglike, wet and furry, about the size of chipmunks. What relief! There were no human features on the little pups at all.

"They're beautiful," I told Maria.

"Bring them out," she said.

Then Ellouise stood up and I saw that there was one more body behind her. It was pale-skinned and hairless. I shined the light upon it and saw that it was not a dog, but a tiny baby boy.

"Oh, God," I said.

"What is it?" said Maria, from above.

I was silent. The little boy, my son, kicked his legs

and let out a high-pitched cry. I dove forward and put my hand over his mouth.

"It's okay," I said.

"Bring them out," said Maria.

"I will," I said.

One by one I scooped up the puppies and delivered them to Maria who stood waiting with a towel. I brought them all to her, all except the boy. While she was inside with the pups, I crawled back under the porch, took off my shirt, and wrapped him up inside it. I placed the boy back in the nest that Ellouise had dug out for the puppies, and left him under the porch.

We made a new nest for Ellouise inside one of the closets and put the puppies there. Ellouise whined in protest, insisting that all her puppies were not with her.

"It's okay, Ellouise," I said.

That night, as Maria slept, I went back under the porch. There, in the little dirt nest I had dug for him, lay my son. He kicked and let out a cry. I cupped him in my hands and smuggled him inside where Ellouise was nursing her pups. She seemed relieved to see him.

I placed the tiny boy's mouth upon one of her nipples and watched as he sucked away at the dog's milk. I examined him more closely in the dim light. He seemed perfectly human, except that he was so small. I could hold him easily in one hand. Perhaps as he grew older his dog features would emerge.

I let the little boy nurse until he'd had his fill, and then I scooped him up again. I lined the inside of a shoebox with one of my old T-shirts and put the child inside. Then I took him for a ride in the car. We drove far out into the countryside and as dawn was breaking we came upon a bridge which passed over a river. At first, I thought I would toss the child over, into the water, but then I decided to do something else.

The sun was beginning to rise and there was a fog on the river's surface. I took my dogchild down to the riverbank, still carrying him in the little shoebox lined with my shirt. The river's current was strong and swift. I walked into the water until it reached past my knees. Then I set the dogchild afloat in his little box. He drifted away from me, spinning on the swirling current. Soon my firstborn son had disappeared into the fog. For a while I just stood there feeling the cool water wrap around my legs and watching a new day emerge. I thought to myself, Maybe some princess will find my child drifting along like that. Maybe she'll raise him as one of her own, and he will be the leader of his people.

PART II

THE MUSKRAT

Maria and I found homes for the remaining pups and then we broke up. It was a mutual decision. She never did find out about my secret. Maria took

Ellouise with her but I kept one of the pups for myself—
I called her Ellouise Jr.—and we moved out to the country. Our relationship was purely platonic.

One morning I let Ellouise Jr. outside and about a
half hour later she returned with what I thought was a
muskrat in her mouth. It was a limp, furry creature
with a long body and short little legs. I assumed it was
dead until she put it down on the kitchen floor and
the little rodent ran under the sofa.

I got a broomstick and tried to coax it out, but the
muskrat wouldn't budge. He was all huddled up in the
corner where I couldn't get in a good poke.

"Okay, fine," I said. I lifted up the couch and moved
it away from the wall. Now he had nowhere to hide. But
when I looked back under there the muskrat was gone.
For a second I thought he had made a run for the door,
but then I realized he had climbed up into the lining of
the couch. I could see a little sag in the fabric where he
was standing.

"Oh, well," I said. I wasn't about to rip up the couch
over a muskrat. I figured I'd just leave my doors open and
hope he had the sense to make an escape sometime soon.

I tried to be especially quiet that morning so as not
to frighten my new houseguest. I put Ellouise Jr. in the
backyard. She was very anxious about the whole thing.
She rarely got the chance to eat live animals and I could
tell she regarded the muskrat's escape as a piece of
pretty bad luck.

The morning passed by and, despite my efforts, the

muskrat stayed where it was. At lunchtime I placed a plate of tuna fish next to the couch hoping the aroma would lure him out, but that didn't work, either.

Then, at about two o'clock that afternoon, I began to hear the singing. It was a tiny, high-pitched voice. First I checked to see if I'd left the radio on at a low volume. Then I looked outside to see if maybe someone far away was singing, but I saw nothing. Eventually I figured out that the sounds were coming from inside the couch. I moved a little closer.

There is a house in New Orleans,
they call the rising sun . . .

The muskrat was singing! And to be fair, he had a fine voice. It was a little timid, and somewhat higher-pitched than what you'd expect, but he could definitely carry a tune.

I knelt down and peered under the couch. "Is that you singing?" I asked

The song stopped.

"It sounded good," I said.

Apparently the muskrat was shy. I shouldn't have said anything at all to him because I didn't hear any more that afternoon.

Later on, though, as I got ready for bed, the singing started up again.

Wake up Little Suzy, wake up . . .

I crept closer to the couch and listened to the whole song. It was a fairly good rendition of the Everly Brothers original. As the song ended I tiptoed into my bedroom and found my old tape recorder. I went back to the couch, ready to get some proof of all this.

I stood there with the tape player in my hand for some time, though. Then I heard, "That's it for tonight, pal."

"Oh, come on," I said.

"That's it."

I stood there a while longer but the muskrat had really meant what he said. That was it for the night.

In the morning, bright and early, I heard that voice again:

Are you going to Scarborough Fair?
Parsley, Sage, Rosemary, and Thyme . . .

I jumped up and began to record the song. When the muskrat was done, I clapped and cheered for more.

"Listen," said the muskrat, "I'd like some more of that tuna fish, if you don't mind."

"Sure," I said. "No problem."

That plate of tuna I had put out for him yesterday was licked clean. He must have snuck out during the night.

I opened up a new can and was feeling really great about all this because now I had it down on tape. I figured the act could be worth a lot of money. I could take it on the road, see the country, me and the singing muskrat. Then I turned around and saw that the little fellow had crawled out from the couch and was tapping his furry paw on my tape player.

"Hey!" I screamed.

He managed to pop the tape out and then he clamped it in his little jaws and scrambled for the open door. He was moving slow because of the weight of the tape, but he still managed to make it outside before I could slam the door shut.

The muskrat leapt down the stairs and started to make his way across the lawn when the dog spotted him and went into hot pursuit. The muskrat made a valiant dash for the woods, but he didn't last long. Ellouise Jr. caught up with him and with one quick shake the little creature went limp.

I ran outside and yelled at her to put him down. I hoped for another recovery like the one yesterday on my kitchen floor, but I guess the dog had decided not to make the same mistake twice. The muskrat fell to the ground and didn't move.

I called Ellouise Jr. off and went over to see what could be done. I reached down to pick up the little virtuoso and was very surprised to see that he wasn't a muskrat after all. The furry pelt had just been a disguise. Wrapped up in this clever rodent coat was actually a tiny little man. Boy, had I been fooled! He'd looked just like a muskrat to me. I removed the costume from this strange fellow and held him up. He was about a foot tall, like a little doll, and there was a tooth mark right through his heart. He had probably died instantly.

Of course, at this point I began to think back on my only other experience with a person who was of diminutive size: my son, the dogchild. Could this have been him? He seemed awfully mature, but perhaps he had aged in dog years. I hugged the little body to my chest and cried.

Later that day I buried him in a shoebox, just like the one that had served as a vessel for my son. As I heaped fresh dirt upon his grave I tried to think of what would compel a person to behave so strangely. Why masquerade as a muskrat? And why hide in my couch like that? Why not share those songs with the world? At least I still had that tape of him singing, and in the years to come I would have a hard time convincing anybody of the truth behind those soulful tunes.

PART III
WENDY

Several months after that singing muskrat incident I received a mysterious package in the mail. I opened it up and inside was an old shirt of mine. It was folded up neatly and pinned to it was a note.

PLEASE CONTACT ME REGARDING THIS SHIRT.
—WENDY

This was the T-shirt I had used to wrap up my dogchild years ago. My full name was written on the inside of the collar. I should have been more careful about that. I called the phone number Wendy had given me and a deep, husky voice answered.

"Hello?" she said.

"I'm calling about the shirt," I said.

"I knew you would," said Wendy. She was breathing very heavily, like she was about to have a fit.

"Are you okay?" I asked her.

"I'm fine," said Wendy.

Wendy gave me her address and I said I'd come over that afternoon. On my way there I thought about what kind of lies I could tell her. I could say I knew nothing about the shirt, that I'd lost it years ago, but then she probably wouldn't tell me how she'd found it.

When I walked into Wendy's house I quickly realized why she had been breathing so heavily over the phone. She was lying inside an iron lung. It was a huge metal tube-shaped machine, the likes of which I had never seen before.

"It does my breathing for me," explained Wendy.

She lay on her back, looking at me through a mirror which was angled above her head so that she could see the whole room. The lung made big hissing and whooshing noises. All that I could see of Wendy was her head. The rest of her was inside that lung. She had smooth skin and her hair was wrapped up in a small white sheet, sort of like a nun's habit. I don't think she had any eyebrows.

"Have a seat," said Wendy.

"Thanks," I said. I sat down in a chair.

Wendy looked me over and smiled. "So you're Victor's father."

"What?" I said.

"I can see the resemblance," said Wendy.

"I don't know what you mean."

"Okay, fine," said Wendy.

I looked around the house. It was nicely decorated. There were little knickknacks, like ceramic dwarves and wooden seagulls, placed on all the windowsills.

"I have not always been in this condition," said Wendy.

"Oh."

"I used to be very active. Three years ago I was swimming alone in a nearby river. I dove off a rock into some dark water. It turned out to be quite shallow and I broke my spine. I would have drowned right there except a small man turned me over and swam me to shore."

Telling that story had taken a lot out of Wendy. Her lung whirred into overdrive to catch up with her lack of breath. Eventually Wendy composed herself and looked up at me with piercing eyes.

"Victor?" I said.

"Yes."

My son saved lives. I couldn't help but feel a little proud. "Victor came to see me," I said.

"He said he would."

"He was dressed up as a muskrat and my dog ate him."

Wendy was quiet. The big lung kept her breathing steady.

"You want a pork chop?" she asked, "My aide left some pork chops in the fridge."

"No, that's okay," I said.

"They're just going to go bad," said Wendy. "Go ahead, take one."

"Okay," I said.

I went to the refrigerator and got out the pork chops. They were cold and covered in grease.

"You need anything?" I asked her.

"I'd like some yogurt," she said.

"Okay," I said. I got out a cup of yogurt and a spoon. I sat down next to Wendy's head and fed her occasional spoonfuls of yogurt while I ate the pork chops. I was pretty hungry and they tasted good.

"Victor liked to sing," said Wendy.

"I know he did," I said. In my shirt pocket I had the tape of him singing.

"Do you have a tape player?" I asked Wendy.

"Yes, I do," she said.

"I think you'll like this."

I popped in the tape and Victor began to sing. Wendy's face lit up.

"Oh, Victor," she said.

"That's him," I said.

"Turn it up," said Wendy.

"Okay," I said.

Victor's tiny voice filled the room. I fed Wendy the rest of the yogurt, making sure to wipe her chin clean with a napkin every few bites. The song ended and Wendy said, "He was a special man."

"Yes, he was," I agreed.

Wendy swallowed hard and said, "I have something to tell you."

"What's that?"

"I'm pregnant with Victor's child."

"Pregnant?" I said.

"You're going to be a grandpa," said Wendy.

"That's great," I said.

I decided not to tell Wendy that Victor's mother was a dog.

"Congratulations," I said.

"You, too," said Wendy.

We sat in Wendy's living room and watched the sun go down outside the window. It cast a nice orange light against the walls.

"Will you tell anybody who the father is?" I asked her.

"No," said Wendy, "I'm going to say it's a child of God."

"That's a good idea."

"Thanks."

Wendy fell asleep and I thought about pulling the plug on her iron lung and then running away. Who would have known? But I didn't do it. I fell asleep in the chair next to her and slept quite well because the sound that iron lung made was very soothing.

PART IV
THE BIRTHING

For a short time, Wendy's unlikely pregnancy remained a secret shared between just the two of us. I made my way over to her place when I could and fed her yogurt and cookies. Inevitably, at some point during the visit, Wendy would ask me to tell her stories about Victor.

"There's not much to tell," I would say.

"Oh, come on."

"Well, there was the time Victor poured cement into the toilet bowl . . ."

"Oh, that Victor!" Wendy would laugh. "Such a practical joker!"

"And then there was that time he fought off a rattle-snake in the backyard . . ."

"That's Victor for you, courage like a lion."

I began telling Wendy long, involved tales about the heroic deeds of little Victor. They would go on for hours and feature valiant Victor battling off herds of feral cats and marauding waterfowl. Wendy really seemed to enjoy the stories and I was disappointed one day when she called to say I should probably stop visiting.

"Why?" I asked her.

"Have you seen the newspapers today?" she said.

I went out and got a paper. Right there, on the front page, was a picture of Wendy smiling away from inside her iron lung. The headline said, MIRACLE MOM.

In the days which followed, newspaper and television reporters invaded her home and asked how such a thing could have happened. Wendy told them it was a child of God, just as she had planned. The story of Wendy's divine pregnancy spread all over the country. She became a sort of national celebrity—"The Virgin Wendy" they called her, or sometimes it was simply "Iron Lung Mom."

Wendy refused all forms of medical treatment. Doctors and midwives alike said the whole thing was going to be a difficult process owing to the presence of that iron lung. They said she should consider checking into a hospital, but Wendy would not have it. She issued a simple statement to the press. It said, "A dirty old manger was good enough for Jesus and Mary."

Wendy had let a doctor examine her early on, just to confirm the pregnancy. The doctor said she was indeed pregnant, and furthermore, he noted, it appeared that she was in fact a virgin. "I see no evidence of sexual activity," he said. Good old Victor was so small he left no traces at all.

I tried to stay in touch with Wendy, but it was difficult now that she was famous. Of course, I couldn't let anyone know how we'd come to be friends, and as the birth grew nearer it became harder and harder for me to contact her. She had developed some kind of close-knit entourage, a bunch of spiritual devotees, all of them apparently convinced that a beautiful savior was going to be born in their midst.

I was sitting home alone one evening when I heard the news on the radio: "The Iron Lung Mom has gone into labor . . ."

I got in my car and drove over to Wendy's place. As I approached the house I saw that it was going to be hard to get anywhere near her. The small home was surrounded by bright lights and TV cameras. Throngs of well-wishers and deeply religious folk lined the street, each of them waiting for news about the birth of the new savior.

I parked my car and waded slowly through the masses. They were saying prayers and burning little heaps of frankincense and myrrh. By the time I reached the doorway of the house it was close to midnight. A bearded man wearing some kind of frock was standing out in front telling everyone to leave their gifts in a pile by the gate. I pushed my old T-shirt—Victor's baby blanket—into his hand.

"Give this to Wendy," I said to him.

"She's very occupied," replied the man.

"Tell her it's from Victor," I said.

The man handed the shirt to a solemn-faced woman who looked me over with a discerning eye. Then she scurried inside.

A few minutes later she was back. She whispered something in the bearded man's ear and he looked down upon me.

"You may enter," he said.

Wendy's house was full of burning candles. There were about a dozen other people inside, all of them dressed in the same sort of uniform, some kind of off-white frock. They looked extremely busy, rushing about with rags and towels in their hands. Above this din of activity rose the *whoosh* and *hiss* of Wendy's big lung.

Wendy saw me and called me over. She was sweating and looked to be in pain.

"Tell me a story about Victor," she said.

"I don't know if we've got time for that," I replied.

"Please," said Wendy. Then she gnashed her teeth and shut her eyes tight.

"Help me!" she cried.

Immediately a flock of attendants zipped to her side. I was shoved out of the way. One of the women peeked her head into the other end of Wendy's lung.

"It's coming!" she yelled.

We all gathered around wide-eyed as Wendy moaned and tried with all her might to give birth. An attendant stood at her side, rubber gloves on his hands, ready to retrieve the baby from inside the iron lung.

A few more tense moments passed and then we heard noises from inside the iron lung—a little squeak and a cry. The attendant reached inside and pulled out a wiggling mass, which he laid on the floor.

The crowd bunched forward and stared down in awe and wonder at the sight before them. A young man said "Good Lord." A woman in front of me fainted. On the carpet before us sat not one, but four small, squirming figures. They were unlikely saviors, to be sure.

"What is this?" someone asked.

"Puppies," I said quietly.

One of the pups barked and took its first breath of air. The others soon followed, yipping away into the night. No one knew what to do. They had not, of course, been expecting this.

"What's going on?" asked Wendy. She couldn't see her newborn pups due to the bulkiness of the lung.

"You had some puppies," I said.

"What?" said Wendy. Her face went white.

One of the attendants scooped up the little dogs and presented them to Wendy. She screamed and passed out on the spot.

"Get an ambulance!" someone yelled.

There was a tremendous clamoring outside. They could hear the puppies barking and wanted to know just what was going on.

The bearded man went outside and made a very brief announcement.

"She had puppies," he said.

Within a few minutes a crew of emergency technicians had burst through the door and whisked Wendy and her four puppies away.

After she was gone all of the frock-clad attendants stood about utterly bewildered. They wandered around disillusioned and speechless. I suppose I could have cleared up a few things for them, but it would only have meant a lot of trouble for me. I slipped away in the dust and confusion.

PART V
FREE TO A GOOD HOME

Wendy didn't last long in the hospital. The trauma and shock were too much for her fragile system and she died shortly after her arrival there. In the days which followed, there was, of course, a lot of speculation about the whole situation. A few pundits and prophets stuck with the assertion that the new messiahs had in fact been born that night. The word "dog" spelled backwards is, after all, "God." But for the most part, people viewed it as some kind of sick prank and the story slowly began to fade from the public eye.

As for Ellouise Jr. and me, we tried to enjoy our life in the country. We took long walks together in the hills and sometimes she would chase after deer or rabbits which would scurry through the bushes and under rocks to avoid her clamping jaws. It was a nice time for me and Ellouise Jr., although we were a little lonely.

One evening I was standing outside the local gas station and a little handmade flyer caught my eye. It said:

FREE TO A GOOD HOME

Underneath those words was a fuzzy picture of some adolescent dogs, four wide-eyed mutts standing in a muddy yard behind a chicken-wire fence. Under the picture the owner had written, "These dogs should stay together."

I looked closer at their eyes. Were these my descendants? It was hard to tell. I wondered who would accept this crew into their home, all four of them together. Probably no one. I found a pen and wrote down the phone number on my hand.

The man who answered the phone was a hunter. He kept a large kennel full of dogs for use out on the trail. His name was Wayne. I asked him why he was giving away those four dogs and he said simply, "They don't hunt."

I got directions to his place and made arrangements to meet up with him the next day, in the afternoon. Unfortunately, when I got out there the dogs were gone.

"A young lady come and took them this morning," Wayne said to me.

"She took them all?" I said.

"Yes, she did," said Wayne. There were dogs all over his property, big barrel-chested huskies roaming free and little ferocious yappers tied to trees with frayed

156

rope. The hunting hounds howled from the rooftops of their small wooden-box homes.

"I don't suppose you know where this woman went," I said.

"No, I don't," said Wayne, "but I hope she doesn't come back. Those were some strange dogs. I was glad to see them go."

"I see," I said.

I looked around at Wayne's collection of canines. They all seemed pretty strange, if you asked me. I wrote down my phone number and address on a piece of paper and handed it to Wayne.

"If that woman does come back," I said, "could you tell her to look me up?"

Wayne took the piece of paper and folded it with his dirty fingers. "I'll give it to her," he said, "if she comes back." And then he went back to his hounds.

A few months later, very late at night, I heard a knocking on my door. Outside there stood a distressed young woman. She was dressed in baggy overalls and her hair was knotted together in long clumps. Her face was white and full of worry.

"Wayne said I should talk to you," she said to me.

"I see," I said. I opened the door and let her inside.

I heated up some water on the stove and made her some tea. Outside, in front of my house, sat a large pickup truck with a homemade wooden camper attached to the back. The woman's name was Delilah and she told me she'd made that camper herself, with her own hands.

"I'd like to talk to you about the dogs," she said.

"Where are they?" I asked her.

"Outside," she said, "in the truck."

I followed her outside and she opened up the door to her wooden camper.

"Wilbur, Pedro, Chetro, Eliza," she said quietly, "we have a visitor."

I heard the dogs rustle about in the camper, groaning and sighing over just being woken up. One of them growled. "It's okay," Delilah said to me, "they don't bite."

I climbed inside the truck. It was cramped and smelled like wet dogs and wool. Delilah turned on a light. There sat four full-grown dogs, each of them perched on their own small mattress. They were brown and spotted, good-looking hounds. They blinked at me in the light.

"Nice dogs," I said to Delilah.

"Yes," she said, "they are."

Delila introduced me to each of them, and then we sat there for a moment—us and the dogs—saying nothing, wondering why we were all there.

Then Delilah said, "It's okay."

The four dogs let out a collective sigh. Wilbur, the largest of the group, kind of coughed. He raised up his head and looked right at me.

"So," he said, "who the hell is this guy?" He had a

strange voice, sort of a cross between a howl and a whine, but it was a voice all the same.

"He knows Wayne," said Delilah.

"Oh, I'm not going back there," said Pedro, the long-haired dog.

"No way," said little Chetro.

Eliza, a beautiful lean hound, shook her head in agreement.

Delilah looked at me and bit her lip.

"When did they learn to talk?" I asked her.

"I don't know," she told me. "I didn't know they could do this. I just wanted some dogs. I don't know how they picked all this up. But I know this isn't right. Most dogs don't do this."

One of the dogs, Chetro, began to tap his paw on the floor. The other dogs joined in, forming a steady, rythmic beat. Then, in those crazy-pitched voices, they began to sing:

Whoa, whoa, whoa, for the longest time . . .

I sat in amazement as they ran through the old Billy Joel original in fine a cappella. They could even harmonize! It was quite an act. But then I looked over at Delilah. Her face was sullen and forlorn.

"What's the matter?" I asked her.

"Something happened," she said.

"What do you mean?"

"I don't know what to do," she said. "I don't know where to go."

I looked around at the dogs. Each of them hung his head. All except big Wilbur. He stared right at Delilah.

"You can tell him," said Wilbur.

"Something happened," said Delilah again.

Eliza lifted her head. In a soft voice, she said to me, "Delilah is pregnant."

Delilah began to cry. Pedro whined a little and Chetro went over and licked her on the cheek.

I looked at each of the dogs. "And who is the father?" I asked them.

Wilbur said, "I am."

I stood up and shuffled closer to Delilah. It was hard to move inside that camper. The ceiling was so low. I got down on my knees and knelt in front of Delilah. She was silent now, her face covered over with all that dread-locked hair. I could see tears dropping from her face onto her lap.

I said to her, "You can stay here, Delilah. It will be okay. We'll take care of this baby together. We'll raise him up as if he were our own."

EPILOGUE
FAMILY

Delilah is eight months pregnant now, large-bellied and happy. We live far out in the countryside with the dogs—the four talkers, and their aunt, Ellouise Junior. These days Delilah and I rarely interact with humans. The dogs are all the company we need. In the evenings we all get together around the fire and tell each other stories, drinking and laughing late into the night. Sometimes the dogs will even treat us to a song or two. Strange as it may seem, I feel as if now I have found a family.

One morning long-haired Pedro came up to me with a dirty cloth bundle in his mouth. He said he had dug it up in the backyard.

"I was wondering if you knew what this is," he asked me.

I unwrapped the bundle and saw that it was little Victor's skeleton. Everything had been pretty well preserved—the tiny golf-ball-sized skull, the thin femurs, and fragile rib cage.

"Yes, Pedro," I said, "I know what this is."

I whistled for the rest of the dogs. They came running home from the woods and fields where they had been playing and stood before me with their long tongues hanging out. Delilah joined them as well, walking slowly, her hands clasped underneath her tremendous, smooth and shiny belly.

"Gather 'round children," I told them all. "I have a story to tell . . ."

Roslyn's Dog

Down the street from me, in a little wood-framed chicken-wire pen, lived Roslyn's dog. She was a short-haired mutt with wild eyes and a hyperactive demeanor which led her to pace back and forth within the small confines of her dirt-lined cage. I passed by Roslyn's dog almost every day as I walked from my house into town. Roslyn had warned me on several occasions not to stick my hand inside that dog's pen.

"She's territorial," explained Roslyn.

"Oh, I understand," I said.

But of course this sort of information only served to pique my interest. One evening, on my way home, I knelt down beside the cage and looked closely at the face of Roslyn's dog. The dog stared back at me, in a lonely sort of way, and soon I found myself talking to her.

"Hello," I said. "How are you?"

Obviously the dog didn't reply, but her passive reaction was enough to make me think that I was welcome there. It occured to me then that maybe Roslyn's dog had been mistreated in the past and all she needed now was a little warmth and affection. I stuck my fingers through the holes in the chicken wire and was pleased when the little hound licked at them in a friendly way. I reached through with my other hand and patted her soft fur.

"You're a nice dog," I told her.

"Let me out," I heard the dog say.

"What?" I asked her.

Roslyn's dog stared back at me blankly.

"What did you say?" I asked her again.

The dog ran her tongue across her nose and pawed at the dirt in front of her.

"Did you just speak to me?" I asked.

But there was no answer from Roslyn's dog. She just looked back at me with a sort of sympathetic confusion.

Well, I thought to myself, maybe it's a good idea.

That cage seemed like a rough place to be locked up all the time and I figured a short supervised recess might be in order. I would return the dog to the cage in just a few minutes.

So I undid the wooden latch and let the dog out. At my urging, she crept forward slowly and peered around at the outside world. Then she walked up to me and sank her teeth deep into my leg.

"Hey!" I yelled.

The little mutt let go of me and ran away. I was shocked, and in no small amount of pain, so I didn't chase after her. I went home and washed out the wound

Roslyn's dog had made. There were four small holes, teeth marks, two in my shin and two in the back of my calf. What an ungrateful dog, I thought.

I went back over to Roslyn's house and told her that I had let her dog out by mistake.

"Oh, you shouldn't have done that," said Roslyn.

"I know that now," I said.

We walked the streets for several hours calling out for the dog but it seemed to be a lost cause. She was nowhere to be found. I offered to buy Roslyn a new dog but she said that was okay, there were many more like her at the pound.

"Good night, Roslyn," I finally said.

"See you later," she said to me.

That night, as I lay in bed, I had vivid dreams about Roslyn's dog. She was dressed up in human clothing and walking about on her two hind legs. Sometimes she was wearing simple work clothes, and other times she would be dressed elegantly, in long-flowing formal gowns, as if she were attending a ball. In my dream, the dog wouldn't pay attention to me, even though I kept calling out to her. When at last she did look my way, I gazed right into her dog eyes and that's when I woke up.

It was late in the day and my hurt leg was tingling and a little numb. I stepped out of bed and was very surprised at what I now saw. There was a patch of hair growing on my leg, right where I had been bitten. When I say hair I don't mean simple leg hair, as is commonly found on human beings. I mean fur, like the kind you find on animals. It was thick, and soft, and brown.

I went into the bathroom and took a shower. I found my razor and shaved the fur off my lower leg. It took me a while because the hair was so thick that it clogged up the blades.

"I'd better see a doctor about this," I said to myself.

I got dressed and went outside. I began to walk over to the health clinic and my leg started to itch. I reached down and felt sharp stubble rising out of my skin. The fur was already starting to grow back.

When I got to the health clinic the receptionist asked me to fill out some papers. She gave me a clipboard and I went to the corner of the room to sit and answer their questions. My leg was really itching now. I rolled up my pants and saw that my ankle was getting hairy as well. The brown hairs were poking through my sock.

The form which the receptionist had given me said, "Please state the reason for your visit."

Underneath that I wrote, "A dog bit me and now there is fur growing on my leg."

I looked at those words for a few seconds. Then I looked at the back of my hands. They were getting hairy now, too. My whole body began to itch and I dropped the pen and walked quickly out of the clinic, trying not to attract anyone's attention.

I ran back to my neighborhood. I went over to Roslyn's house and knocked on her door, but she wasn't home. I sat down on her porch and waited for her there. A few hours passed by and I fell asleep where I was. It got dark out and still Roslyn did not return.

Then, as I lay there growing hairier and more uncomfortable by the minute, I felt a familiar tongue lick at my fingertips. It was Roslyn's dog.

"Hey," I said to her, "what is going on here?"

I sat up and the hound looked at me carefully. There was a light coating of fur on my face now, like peach fuzz. Roslyn's dog placed her paws on my knees and drew her long snout up close to me. I heard a voice then, just like the one I thought I'd imagined before.

It said, "Kiss me."

"Kiss you?" I said.

Roslyn's dog pressed closer and I puckered my lips. We kissed for several minutes, our tongues wrapping awkwardly around one another. I reached up and began to stroke her fur. It came off in clumps in my hands. Great fistfuls of it fell to the floor around us. Roslyn's dog began to grow in my arms. Her bony legs filled with flesh and that long snout receded. Her sharp teeth melted down into small white cubes and her floppy ears shrunk into hardened human semicircles.

Soon I was kissing a woman, and that woman pulled away from me. She was naked, and a little hairier than most of the other naked women I've seen, but she was definitely a woman.

She wiped her mouth and coughed a little. "Thank you," she said to me.

I looked down at my hairy hands. They were crumpled up now into big clumsy canine paws. My tongue was so long it barely fit in my mouth. I tried to speak, hardly able to form the words.

"What about me?" I finally said.

The woman nodded and stroked the fur on my head knowingly. Then she placed a collar around my neck. She led me gently down the porch steps—now I was walking on all fours—and we made our way across the packed dirt of Roslyn's yard. She led me to the small chicken-wire cage and put me inside. She patted my fur again and said "thank you" a few more times. Then she left me there with a bowl of dry kibble and water.

In the morning, Roslyn returned to see me. She refilled my bowl with water and scratched at my ears in a familiar way. I wondered then if she knew who I was. I ran in circles, barking loudly, trying to help her see what had happened while she was away. I jumped in the air and pushed my muddy paws against her legs. It was all that I could do. Roslyn smiled down at me and brushed the dirt off her pants. Was I just the same old dog to her?

"It's good to see you again," she said to me. And then she turned around, shut the door to my pen, and walked back into to her house.

She feeds me every day now, and I am always glad to see her come walking down the path my way, just as I would be very glad to see you, should you ever want to stop by and play.